March 5th, 2020;

Everything has changed. I woke up this morning and the world is fundamentally different. People who are very clearly dead are still walking and talking as if they are themselves. How is this possible? Their grey eyes are just as confused as mine.

What happened?

Writer/Letterer - Laurie Calcaterra

Pencils/Inks - Marco Defillo

Colors - Matt D. Chambers III

Editor - Rachael Bulock

10YA (10 YEARS INTO APOCALYPSE)

IT'S TOO QUIET.
EASY, GIRL.
FWOOSH
CLACK

GASP!
HIT IT.
TAP
ALIVE!
KID, DO YOU KNOW THE WAY TO I-93?
WEST OF HERE.
THANKS.

SIGH.
CRACKLE
SO
BEAUTIFUL.
SNAP

GROWL
WHERE ARE YOU?
NIIIIICE, DOGGIES.
GRRRRR
OH SHIT. YOU BROUGHT FRIENDS.
RAAA
SWOOSH
C'mon!
AWOOOO
WHERE DO YOU THINK YOU'RE GOING?!
AWOOOOOOO
WHINNY!
CHICKEN SHITS!

ZZZZZ ...
YAWN
JUST A BIT FURTHER, GIRL.
THEN WE CAN REST.
GROAN.

HELLO, MA'AM. I DON'T MEAN TO STARTLE YOU.
I'M LOOKING FOR SANTA CLAUS.
NOT THE LEGEND, MA'AM, THE TOWN.
AREN'T YOU TOO OLD TO BELIEVE IN SUCH THINGS?

AND WHAT TAKES YOU TO THIS TOWN?

I'M LOOKING FOR DWAYNE FINK. YOU FAMILIAR?
SORRY, I CAN'T HELP YOU ON EITHER ACCOUNT.
THERE WAS A TOWN UP THE BLUFF, BUT I'M NOT SURE IF IT'S STILL THERE.

BEFORE I HEAD OUT, CAN YOU HELP A TRAVELER?
HMPFT.
SARA, DO NOT GET TOO CLOSE.
HELLO, MR.
MY NAME IS JUDE ST. CLAIR, MISS.
CAN I GIVE YOUR HORSEY A CARROT?
I'M SURE HE WOULD PREFER AN APPLE, BUT ALL I HAVE IS CARROTS.

PRINCE IS ACTUALLY A GIRL. HER FULL NAME IS DIANA PRINCE.
SHE IS NAMED AFTER A WARRIOR WOMAN WHO PROTECTS THE HUMAN RACE.
OOOOO.
HELLO, DIANA! WE'LL GET YOU LOTS OF CARROTS FOR THE ROAD.
TSK.
PFFFFT.

TEE-HEE!

HERE YOU ARE TRAVELER, HAVE A SAFE TRIP.
MA'AM.

BYE, MR. JUDE!

WHAT DO YOU THINK, GIRL?
CRACK
BOOM
NICKER
I KNOW, I KNOW WE'VE COME SO FAR...

...BUT, BEAR?
DEAD
CAUTION
BEAR
WHINNY
OK, WE JUST HAVE TO BE QUIET.
I WAS SAVING THESE FOR A SPECIAL OCCASION, BUT TODAY IS THE DAY.
HOPE YOU ENJOY YOUR NEW SNEAKERS!
AND I'VE GOT JUST THE THING.
HAPPY EARLY BIRTHDAY, GIRL.
SNORT

WHAT'S THIS?
LET GO!
GASP!

NO!
PHEW!
...LET'S SEE WHAT WE FOUND.
VEGAS?
Las Vegas
NOW...
CAAAAAAW

WHAT WAS I THINKING?
THAT WAS SO STUPID.
ALL THAT RISK FOR ONE GLASS.
I NEED MORE SLEEP.
CAAAW
I HAVE A BAD FEELING ABOUT THIS.
SHIT.
RLLL?

WHISPER
CAAAW
CRUNCH

SIGH.
!!
TRIP
LAS VEGAS
NO.

CRASH

ROAR

GRAARRR!
LET'S GO, PRINCE!
RUN, GIRL!
GRR GRR
FASTER!
RAWR!
WE'RE NOT GOING TO --
GRRAAA
SLASH
NOOO!

GRAAAAAH
THUMP
Hurk
MrrrrrUMPH
NO!
EEEEEEE!
NOOOOOOO....

GROAN.
OUCH--
I'M TOO OLD FOR THIS SHIT.
PRINCE? WHERE ARE YOU, GIRL?
GASP!

SOB
PRINCE--
THIS IS ALL MY FAULT.

SOB
GOTTA KEEP GOING.
PICK UP...
...THE PIECES.
BECAUSE...
...THE ANSWER IS OUT THERE.
AND I'M GOING TO FIND IT.
NO MATTER THE COST.
GOODBYE...
...PRINCE.
SNIFF.

SIIIIGH.
YOU HAD BETTER BE WORTH IT, DWAYNE.
No Deads
SANTA CLAUS NEXT EXIT

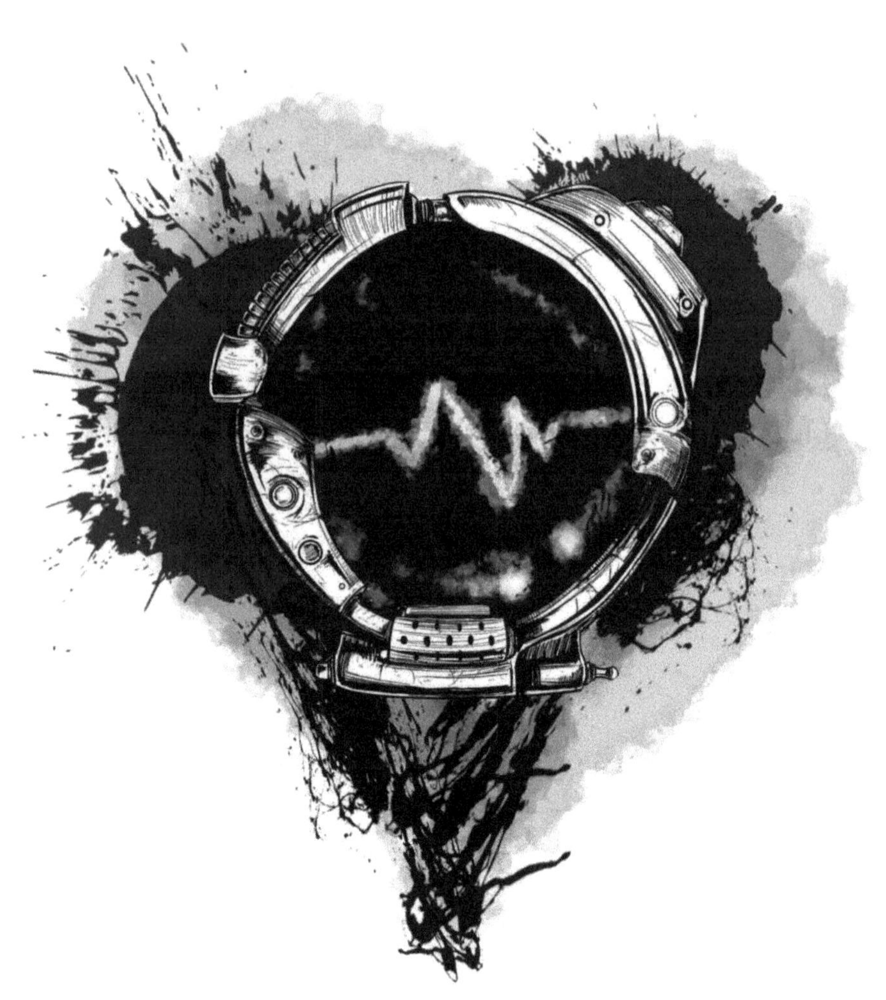

April 25th, 2020:

More info keeps coming. We knew day 1 that people are affected by this. But now animals and insects, too. Death is broken. I wish I knew what happened. Virus? Food contaminated? Chemicals in the water? How is it that there is no more death, only decay?

Writer, Letterer: Laurie Calcaterra

Pencils, Inks, Colors: Marco Defillo

Editor: Rachael Bulock

All Dead HANG
Gaaaa
Help me!
Gurgle...
TWITCH
SANTA SALOON
Welcome
CLINK
CREAK
Welcome

LOOK ALIVE, BARKEEP, YOU GOT A STRANGER.

YESSIR, SHERIFF.
'SCUSE ME.

DID B.J. GETCHA?
BIG JAMES THE BEAR.
BETWEEN THE ROCKSLIDES AND B.J., WE DON'T GET MANY NEWBIES COMING UP I-93.
YOU MUST HAVE A POWERFUL REASON TO BE HERE.
B.J.?
I HAVE BEEN LOOKING EVERYWHERE FOR SOMEONE VERY IMPORTANT.

IMPORTANT YOU SAY? PRAY TELL, WHO ARE THEY?

HIS NAME IS DWAYNE FINK AND HE HAS SUBSTANTIAL INFORMATION.
YOU HEARD OF HIM?

TODAY'S YOUR LUCKY DAY, STRANGER. DWAYNE IS RIGHT THERE.

LET ME GET THIS STRAIGHT, DWAYNE.
THE MAN OF GOLD FOUND THE FOUNTAIN OF YOUTH?
HEH.
NO, JIMMY. GOLD LIVES FOREVER BECAUSE HE SNARED DEATH.
PSHT.
HOW OLD DID YOU SAY HE WAS AGAIN?
HEH.
LEMME SEE NOW...
...HE'S ATLEASTA 102.
NO! 103.
WATCH IT!

I SMELL BULLSHIT.
NO!
YOU SEE, GOLD LIVES IN A PALACE OF LIES WHILE WE FILL THE WORLD WITH THE UNDEAD!
WE ARE BEING JUDGED!
CAREFUL, DWAYNE.
THE WRATH OF GOD 'TIS UPON US!
I'M TELLIN YA, HE KNOWS THE ANSWER TO WHERE DEATH WENT AND --
DAMMIT, DWAYNE!
Auaaaaaaaa!

ALRIGHT NOW, DWAYNE. THIS HAPPENS EVERY TIME YOU GET ALL EXCITED.
LET'S GO SLEEP IT OFF IN THE DRUNK TANK.
OW, MEH HERD HURTZ.

ARE YOU SURE DWAYNE IS THE IMPORTANT PERSON YOU'RE LOOKING FOR?
THE THINGS I HAVE TO DO FOR INFORMATION.
NOTHING.
WHAT'S THAT?

SIGH.
HOW ABOUT ANOTHER DRINK, STRANGER?
I COULD USE MORE LIQUID COURAGE.
C'MON, DWAYNE. UP YOU GET.
MFFRM... GOLD KNOWS, SHERIFF. GOLD.
YOU GUYS NEED ONE MORE?
HUMPH.
THIS SEAT IS EMPTY.
WHERE YOU COME FROM?
WE DON'T CARE.
I WAS ON I-93 AND --

WE DON'T LIKE STRANGERS HERE IN SANTA CLAUS.
YOU NEED TO MOVE ON.
LOOK, I DON'T MEAN NO HARM. I JUST--
I DON'T CARE IF YOU RODE INTO TOWN WITH A BUS FULL OF NUNS.
GET LOST.
I JUST WANT TO PLAY CARDS.
C'MON, JIMMY. LET HIM PLAY.
YEAH, JIMMY. LET ME PLAY.

LET'S GO.
I FOLD.
CALL.
I RAISE.
READ 'EM AND WEEP, BOYS!
SORRY, MA'AM. THIS ONE IS MINE.
GRRR.
DIDN'T I SAY NO STRANGERS?
DON'T BE AN ANIMAL, JIMMY.
SPEAKING OF ANIMALS, WHAT HAPPENED TO YOUR EYE, JIMMY? DID BIG JAMES GIVE YOU A MATCHING SCAR?
THREE OF A KIND!
YOU'LL NEED TO KEEP ON YOUR TOES HERE...
...OR YOU'LL LOSE MORE THAN YOUR MONEY.
NO, STRANGER. I GAVE BIG JAMES HIS.

IS THAT A THREAT?
YOU BET YOUR SORRY ASS, IT IS.
TOO RICH FOR MY TASTE.
I'M OUT. I'M BROKE.
D O U C H E B A G

JUST A WORD OF ADVICE. REMEMBER WHOSE TABLE YOU'RE SITTING AT.

NOW SHUT UP AND PUT UP. IF YOU GOT THE BALLS.
ALL IN.
YOU CAN'T BLUFF YOUR WAY OUT OF THIS ONE, YOU GRIZZLED REDNECK.

I'VE BEEN WATCHIN YOUR TELLS, JIMMY. YOU DON'T HAVE SHIT.

THAT'S THE THING ABOUT TELLS, STRANGER. SOMETIMES THEY AIN'T THE TRUTH.
STRAIGHT FLUSH.

THAT'S ALL MY MONEY!
SHIT!*
THANK YOU FOR YOUR DONATION TO THE SANTA CLAUS CHRISTMAS FUND!
*AMERICAN SIGN LANGUAGE

I GOTTA SAY, STRANGER, I ENJOYED TAKING YOUR MONEY.

NOW GET YOUR ASS OUT OF MY TOWN.

YEAH, I'LL MOVE ON IN THE MORNING.
NO, YOU GO RIGHT NOW!
SCRAPE

I JUST LOST MY HORSE TO A GIANT UNDEAD BEAR AND YOU JUST TOOK ALL MY MONEY.
WHERE AM I SUPPOSED TO GO, JIMMY?
DON'T KNOW.

DON'T KNOW...

...OR DON'T CARE?

PICK ONE.

THAT'S WHAT I THOUGHT. PUNK.
AW, FUCK IT.
KRAKK
PTOO!
SMASH
FOUR ON ONE?! LET'S CHANGE THE ODDS!
FLIP

PLOF
AA AAA!
BLOCK
KRAKK
OOF!
GYAAAAAAAGH!!
WHAM

PHEW! I GOT OFF EASY.
OH, FUUUUU--
PTOOOIE!
GET 'EM!
KRAKK
FIGHT, FIGHT, FIGHT!
STAY DOWN!
SMASH
GRRRR!
KICK

YOU SON OF A BITCH!
CLICK
WHO'S THE BITCH NOW?!
I--

OK, STRANGER, PUT THE GUN DOWN.
NOW SLIDE IT TO ME NICE AND SLOW.
SHHHHHHH
TAP
I'M GONE FOR FIVE MINUTES AND YOU GUYS DESTROY THE PLACE.
THIS IS WHY WE CAN'T HAVE NICE THINGS, FELLAS!
I AM DISAPPOINTED.

THIS IS WHAT YOU GET, ASSHOLE!
SHUT UP, JIMMY. MY GUT TELLS ME YOU STARTED THIS MESS.
YOU CAN CLEAN UP AND GO HOME.
YOU, SIR, HAVE EARNED YOURSELF A NIGHT BEHIND BARS.
WE ONLY HAVE ONE CELL.
AT LEAST YOU'LL HAVE COMPANY.
COMPANY I'M DYING TO MEET.

IF I
UNCUFF YOU,
ARE YOU GOING
TO CAUSE MORE
PROBLEMS?

NO, SIR. I'M PRETTY TIRED OF TROUBLE.
GOOD. NOW TAKE THE EVENING TO THINK ABOUT WHERE YOU'RE GOING IN THE MORNING.
YOU CAN'T STAY HERE. JIMMY WILL LYNCH YOU FOR SURE.
YESSIR, SHERRIFF.
I HOPE THE MORNING HAS ANSWERS TO A LOT OF THINGS.
AFTER YEARS OF SEARCHING, I FINALLY FOUND YOU...
...DWAYNE FINK.
ZZZZ

PSSSSSSS...

PSSSSSSSS

I WISH I COULD UNSEE THAT.

OH MY GATOS!
I DIDN'T SEE YA THERE.

YOU DIDN'T SEE ME WHILE YOU WERE PISSING NEXT TO MY HEAD?
NOPE.

I DON'T GET CELLMATES.
WHATCHA IN FER?

I'VE BEEN SEARCHING FOR YOU FOR FIVE YEARS, DWAYNE.

ME? YOU'VE BEEN LOOKING FOR ME?!
WHY?

BECAUSE YOU KNOW HOW THIS ALL STARTED. DON'T YA?
NO ONE BELIEVES ME WHEN I TELL THEM.
DO YOU REMEMBER WHEN YOU SAW YOUR FIRST ONE?

FOR ME, IT ALL STARTED WITH FREDERICK NEEDLEMEYER.
1YA (1ST YEAR OF APOCALYPSE)
and as her young man dies
on a cold and gray Chicago mornin'
I LOVE ELVIS!
another little baby child is born...
...in the ghetto
AND HIS MOMMA CRIED.
OH SHIT —
KABOOM

WHEOOOWH- WHEOOO
AiEEEEEEEEE BANG
NOOOO HELP
Smash
COUGH ACK
BOOM

WHEEOP-WOOP- WOOP-
OH GOD, OH GOD, OH--

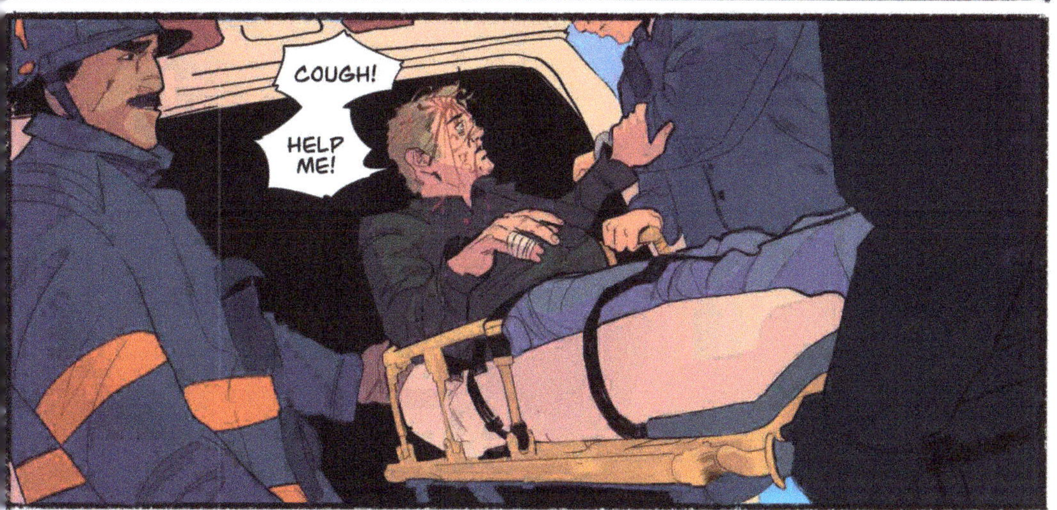

COUGH!
HELP ME!

IT'S OK, SIR. I'M JUDE, AN EMERGENCY CARE PROVIDER.
I'M HERE TO HELP.
JUD
TO BE CONTINUED...

May 10th, 2020;

Things are getting tight. Meat is scarce because cows apparently don't like to be butchered any more than kids like eating burgers that move. Vegetable farmers can't use pesticides to keep insects away. I read someone tried to light a swarm on fire and burnt his whole farm down. People aren't prepared for this. Hungry people make bad decisions.

Writer/Letterer - Laurie Calcaterra
Pencils/Inks - Marco Defillo
Colors - Matt D. Chambers III
Editor - Rachael Bulock

WHAT'S YOUR NAME?
THAT'S GOOD FRED. DO YOU KNOW YOUR BLOODTYPE?
F-F-FRED.
IT'S A POSITIVE.
MARCH 5TH, 2020
1ST DAY OF APOCALYPSE
AMBULANCE

AARON, WE HAVE A+, RIGHT?
FREDERICK A. NEEDLEMEYER.

DRIVER LICENSE
YES, JUDE. WE HAVE A+.

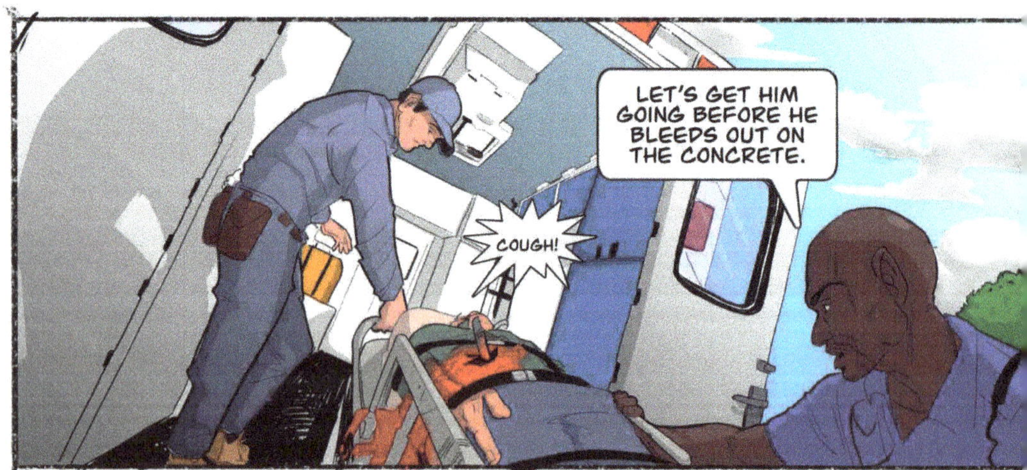

LET'S GET HIM GOING BEFORE HE BLEEDS OUT ON THE CONCRETE.
COUGH!

CARLOS, LET'S GO!
I'M ON IT, JEFE!

STARTING IV.
GUYS... IS IT BAD? AM I --

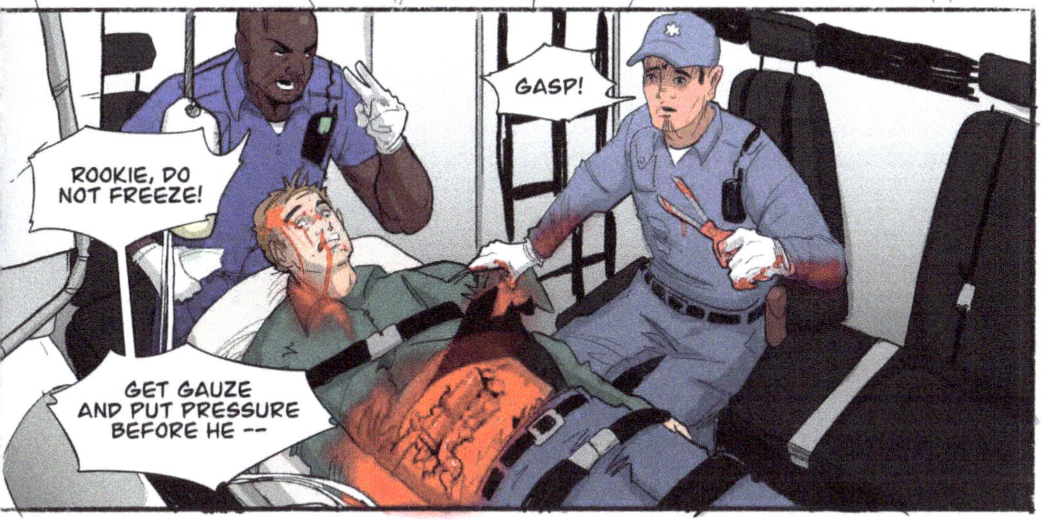

GASP!
ROOKIE, DO NOT FREEZE!
GET GAUZE AND PUT PRESSURE BEFORE HE --

HURK

PREP THE DEFIBRILLATOR, HE'S GOING TO NEED A JOLT!
BZZZ

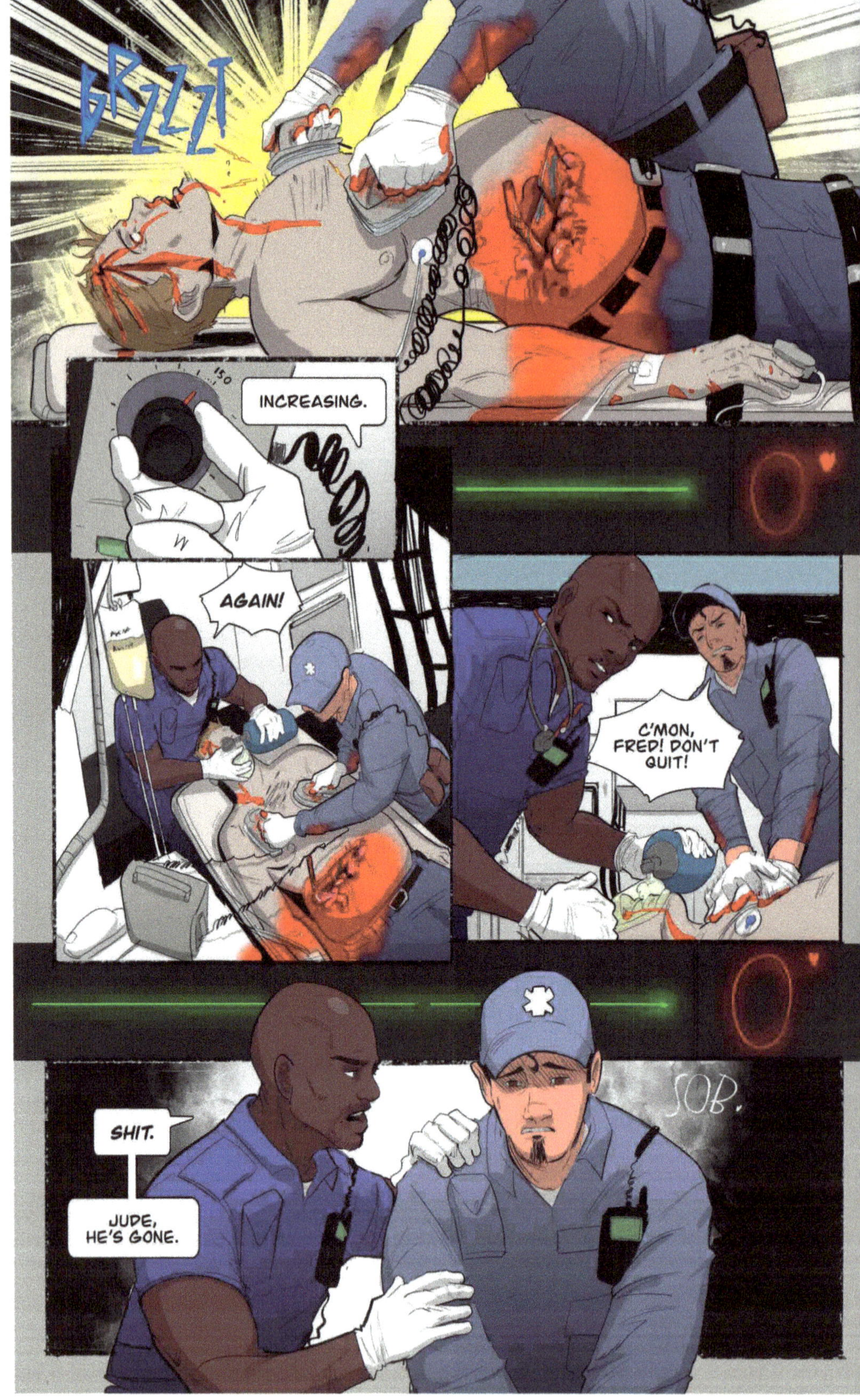
GRZZZT
INCREASING.
AGAIN!
C'MON, FRED! DON'T QUIT!
SOB.
SHIT.
JUDE, HE'S GONE.

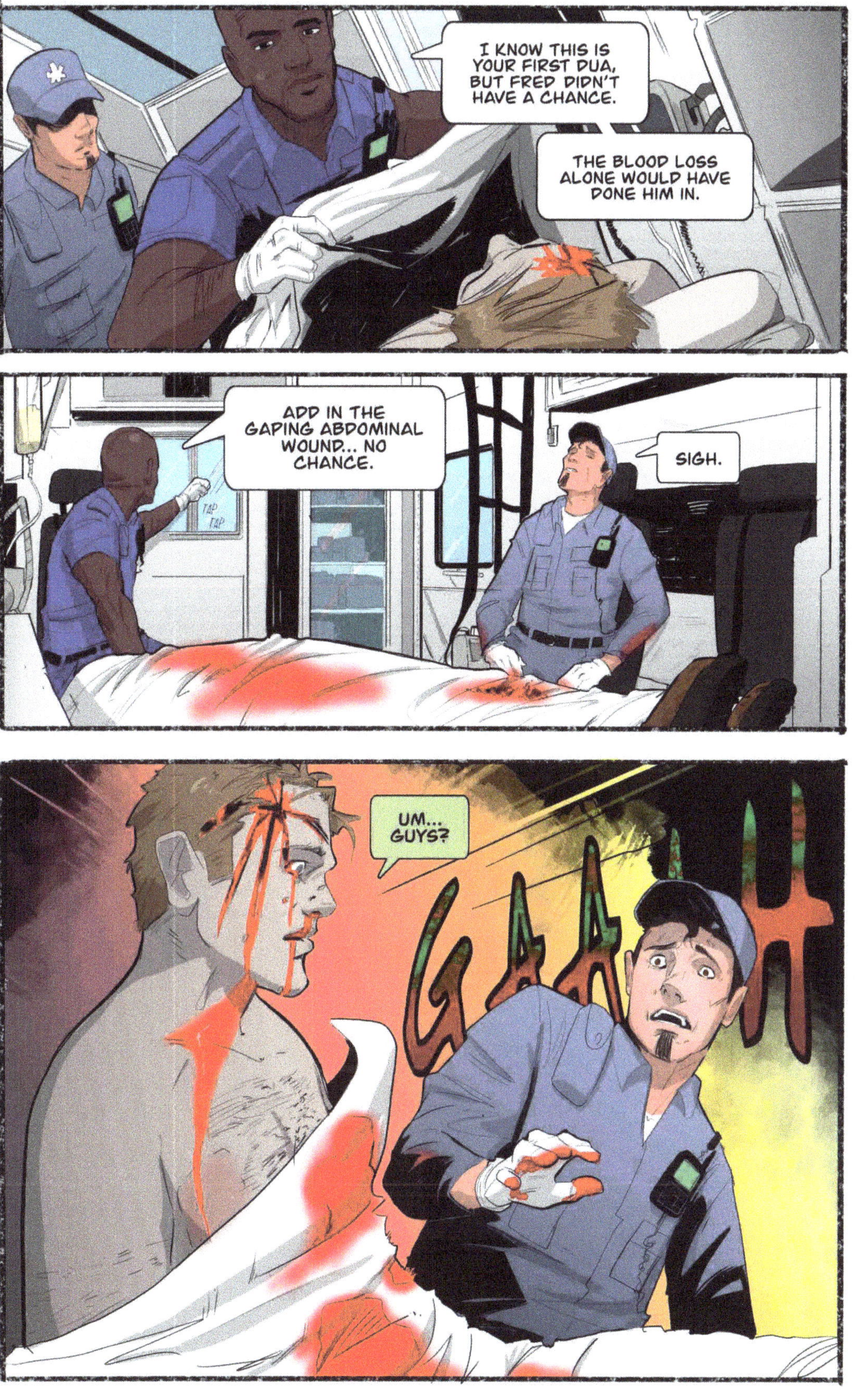

I KNOW THIS IS YOUR FIRST DUA, BUT FRED DIDN'T HAVE A CHANCE.
THE BLOOD LOSS ALONE WOULD HAVE DONE HIM IN.

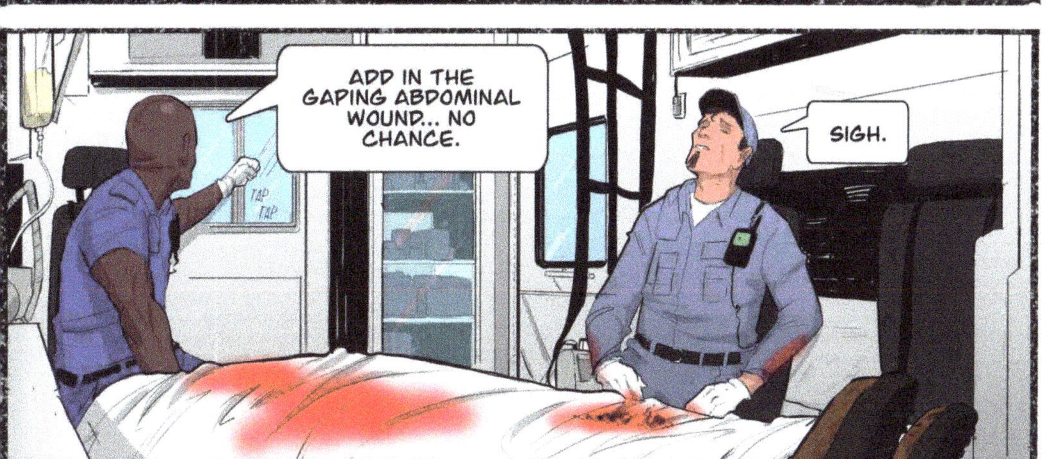

ADD IN THE GAPING ABDOMINAL WOUND... NO CHANCE.
SIGH.
TAP TAP

UM... GUYS?
GAAAH

HELLO, I'M DR. CARMICHAEL.
I AM THE ATTENDING DOCTOR TODAY AND I'VE BEEN THROUGH THIS CHART THREE TIMES.
KNOCK KNOCK
ACCORDING TO THIS, AT 09:27 THE PATIENT EXSANGUINATED, CAUSING HEART ARRHYTHMIA AND FAILURE.
BUT HERE HE SITS. WHO FILLED OUT THIS REPORT?
I DID, DOC.
JUDE ST. CLAIR, YOU HAVE BEEN A FIRST RESPONDER FOR THREE WEEKS.
I UNDERSTAND THAT IS A SHORT TIME, BUT I EXPECTED BETTER THAN THIS.
MR. NEEDLEMEYER, IF I AM READING THIS CHART CORRECTLY, IT STATES YOU DIED TWO HOURS AGO. CAN YOU EXPLAIN THIS?
SIGH... IT'S TOO EARLY FOR PRACTICAL JOKES, AARON.

DOC, MAYBE YOU SHOULD EXAMINE THE PATIENT. WOULD YOU LIKE TO USE MY STETHOSCOPE?
NO, THANK YOU. I'LL USE MY OWN.

I'M NOT FALLING FOR YOUR TRICK.

WHAT THE --

EQUIPMENT MALFUNCTION?
TAP TAP
TAP TAP

OK, AARON. LET ME TRY YOURS.

STILL NOTHING? NO HEARTBEAT?!

HEY DOC, MAYBE YOU CAN HELP ME FIGURE THIS OUT?

DEAR GOD!
I DUNNO, BUT THIS COULD BE PART OF THE PROBLEM.
FLOP
OKAY...
... I'M SURE THERE IS A... PERFECTLY LOGICAL EXPLAINATION.
AND I WILL GO FIND IT!
WAIT HERE!
CRASH
FIVE DOLLARS SHE'S NOT COMING BACK.
NO TAKERS.

DAD? I'M HOME!
SIGH.
WHAT A CRAZY DAY.
CLINK

JUST... UNBELIEVABLE.

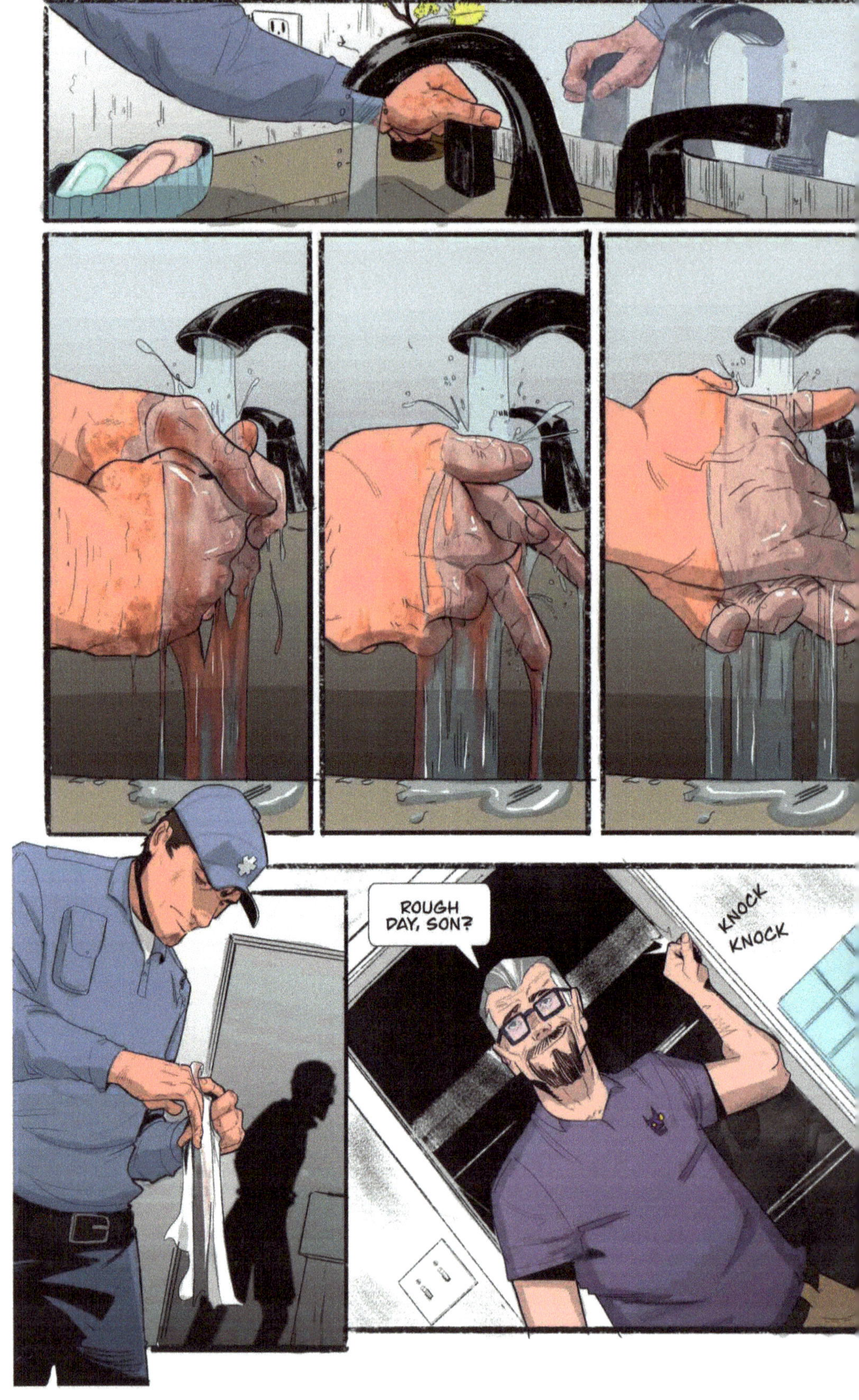
ROUGH DAY, SON?
KNOCK KNOCK

YOU COULD SAY THAT.
THERE WAS A SIX CAR PILE UP ON I-75 TODAY.
HAVE A SEAT AND WE CAN TALK ABOUT IT. MOM MADE YOU A PLATE.

THANKS, MOM

I SAW THE CRASH ON TV TODAY. WHAT HAPPENED?
ASL

I WAS CALLED TO A SCENE WHERE A SIXTEEN WHEELER WIPED THE ROAD AND EVERYONE ON IT. IT WAS GRUESOME.

THE GUY WE PICKED UP NEVER HAD A CHANCE.
WE WATCHED HIM DIE, BUT SOMEHOW HE CAME BACK.
THE HOSPITAL SENT HIM HOME. I'M STILL TRYING TO FIGURE OUT WHAT HAPPENED.

YOU RESCUCITATED HIM?
Man with no heartbeat

NO, IT WAS SOMETHING ELSE.
THE WORST PART WAS WHEN THE DOCTOR PANICKED.
SIGH... I JUST NEED TO SLEEP AND GET MY HEAD RIGHT.
THANKS FOR THE SANDWICH.

HE WILL BE FINE. IT'S NEW. LET HIM ADJUST.
I TOLD YOU. IT'S TOO MUCH FOR HIM.

...and then this truck smashed everything on the road.
I got hurt pretty bad. The guys tried to save me, I remember that much.
But the hospital didn't know what to do and sent me home.
I think I died? I have a huge wound. Want to see?
Good evening. We at WDED 13 have breaking news about the ongoing crisis.
As we continue to hear more and more cases of humans affected by the undead condition...
THE LIVING DEAD
LOUIS LANDON
... it has come to our attention that animals are also included in this phenomenon.
owing video contains violent images.
LOUIS LANDON
Viewer discretion is advised.

This footage has not been edited or altered.
REC
LOOK, LARRY! THERE'S A GIANT ONE. DON'T MISS.
BANG
I GOT HIM, MARK.
SHRIEK
GRRRRR
OH SHIT!
REC
ROARFFF
AAIEE
REC
GURGLE
GROWL
NO!
REC
ROAR
REC
HELP ME!

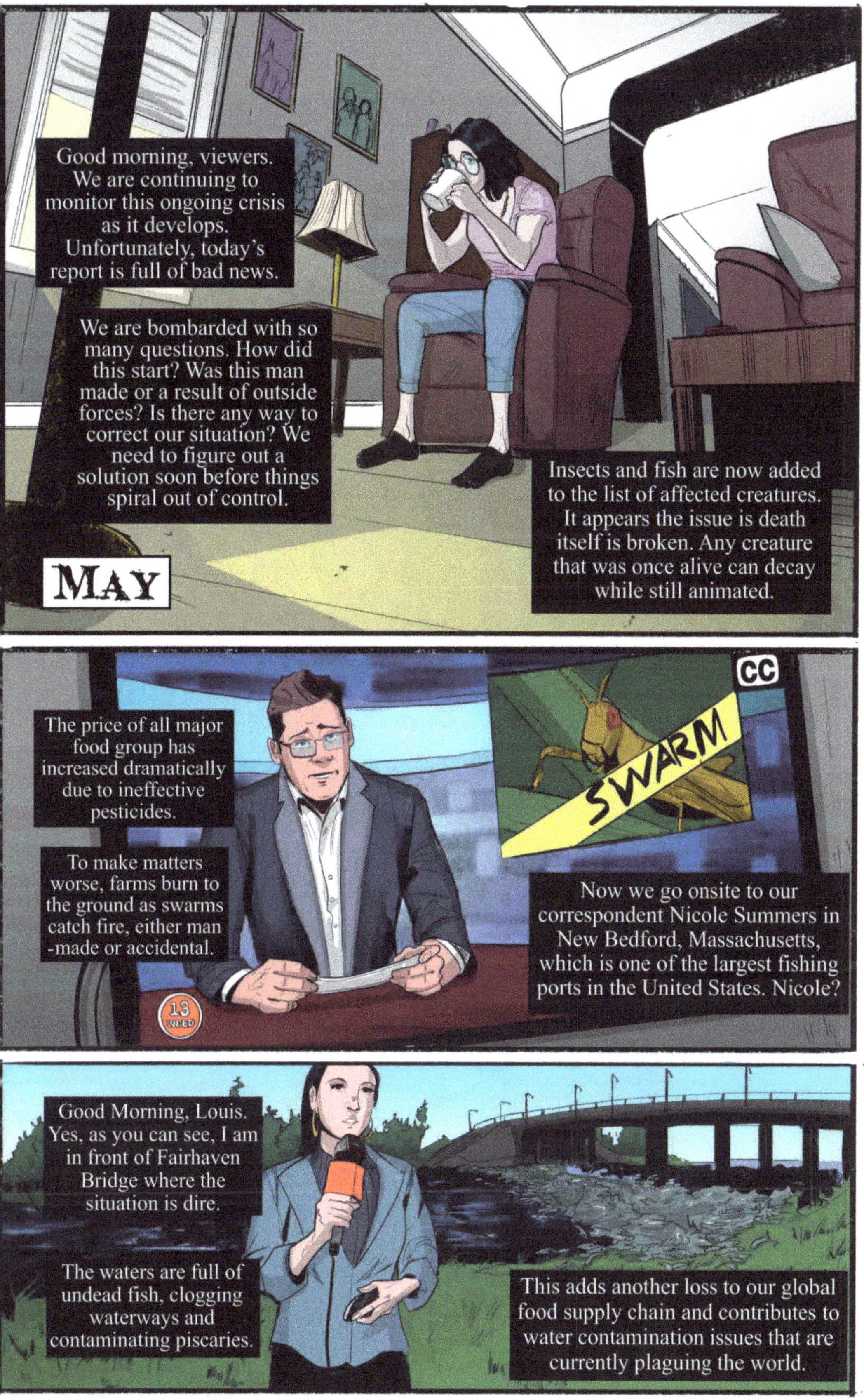

Good morning, viewers. We are continuing to monitor this ongoing crisis as it develops. Unfortunately, today's report is full of bad news.
We are bombarded with so many questions. How did this start? Was this man made or a result of outside forces? Is there any way to correct our situation? We need to figure out a solution soon before things spiral out of control.
MAY
Insects and fish are now added to the list of affected creatures. It appears the issue is death itself is broken. Any creature that was once alive can decay while still animated.
The price of all major food group has increased dramatically due to ineffective pesticides.
To make matters worse, farms burn to the ground as swarms catch fire, either man-made or accidental.
SWARM
CC
13 WDED
Now we go onsite to our correspondent Nicole Summers in New Bedford, Massachusetts, which is one of the largest fishing ports in the United States. Nicole?

Good Morning, Louis. Yes, as you can see, I am in front of Fairhaven Bridge where the situation is dire.
The waters are full of undead fish, clogging waterways and contaminating piscaries.
This adds another loss to our global food supply chain and contributes to water contamination issues that are currently plaguing the world.

SEPT
As the living wonder where our next meal is coming from…
BREAKING NEWS
…violent encounters involving the Undead have increased 435%.
THMP!
FREEZE!
Something needs to be done about this wave of violence.
LET ME GO!
DETROIT   DET. PD
24601 OCT 30 2020
DOB 7 4 1979
DOD 8 11 2020
GRANT, C.A.

JUDE, DID YOU SEE THIS? THEY JUST PASSED A NATIONAL CURFEW FOR THE UNDEAD.
THAT'S NOT GOING TO GO OVER WELL.
Good evening, Landon.
CC
2YA

We are standing outside of the Dallas courthouse after the decision for -

OH MY-
BANG!

GASP!
Governments around the world are passing new laws regarding the "Living Impaired" with promises for additional legislation.
With the amount of negative attention the Undead are receiving, I predict that these curfews are just the beginning.

Good evening. This is day 9 of the nationwide riot in response to phase one "Protect the Living" law being rolled out by the Federal Government.
We have been ordered to shelter in place as this unrest unfolds across major cities everywhere. God help us.
911

Breaking news: All citizens are required to wear this new technology.
3YA
Let me introduce you to "The Disc".

All citizens must allow the disc to be activated by law enforcement to determine if a heartbeat is present.
DID I READ THAT RIGHT? REQUIRED?
THIS LOOKS UNCOMFORTABLE.

IT'S THE LEAST WE CAN DO TO MAINTAIN ORDER.
IT FEELS WEIRD, THOUGH.

I DON'T WANT TO BE MISTAKEN FOR UNDEAD.
WHAT IF IT RUNS OUT OF BATTERIES?

CC
Phase 2 of "Protect the Living" law has been rolled out with the creation of the "Undead Collection Unit".
ЧYA
FREEZE, LADY!

Per the new law, Undead will be separated from living communities for the safety of all.
SOB
WAIT! PLEASE DON'T TAKE HER!

MOMMA, I'M SCARED!

SHE'S. ONLY FIFTEEN, SHE ISN'T A THREAT!
THIS IS FOR THE GOOD OF THE COMMUNITY, MA'AM.
WHAT IS WRONG WITH YOU?! SHE'S A LITTLE GIRL!

BAM
OOF!

NO! STACEY!
MOMMA!

EMPTY AGAIN. THESE SHORTAGES ARE TERRIBLE.
5YA

GLUTEN-FREE BEER? GROSS.

WELP, LET'S SEE IF ANYONE HAS FIGURED OUT THE "WHY" YET.
GRAWR

WDED 13 STILL ON?
click

THE GOVERNMENT KNEW THE GREYS WERE COMING AND DID NOTHIN!
DO YOU HAVE PROOF OF GOVERMENT COVER UP?
13 WDED
Aliens to blame?

ALIENS?

CLICK!
When it comes to an inspired and privileged retirement, Pine Fox is where you want to be.
Pine Fox Undead Retirement Community
WHERE BEING UNDEAD IS EASY.
For more information, call (216) 555-3323 today!
CADY, TIME TO COME IN.
CLICK!
AND I SAY TO THEE...
...REPENT! HEAVEN IS FULL AND WE HAVE BEEN ABANDONED BY GOD!
Possible religious event?

SIGH... FIVE YEARS AND WE STILL HAVE NO CLUE WHAT CAUSED THIS.
SLEEP TIGHT, MOM.

I LOVE YOU.
SEE YOU IN THE MORNING.

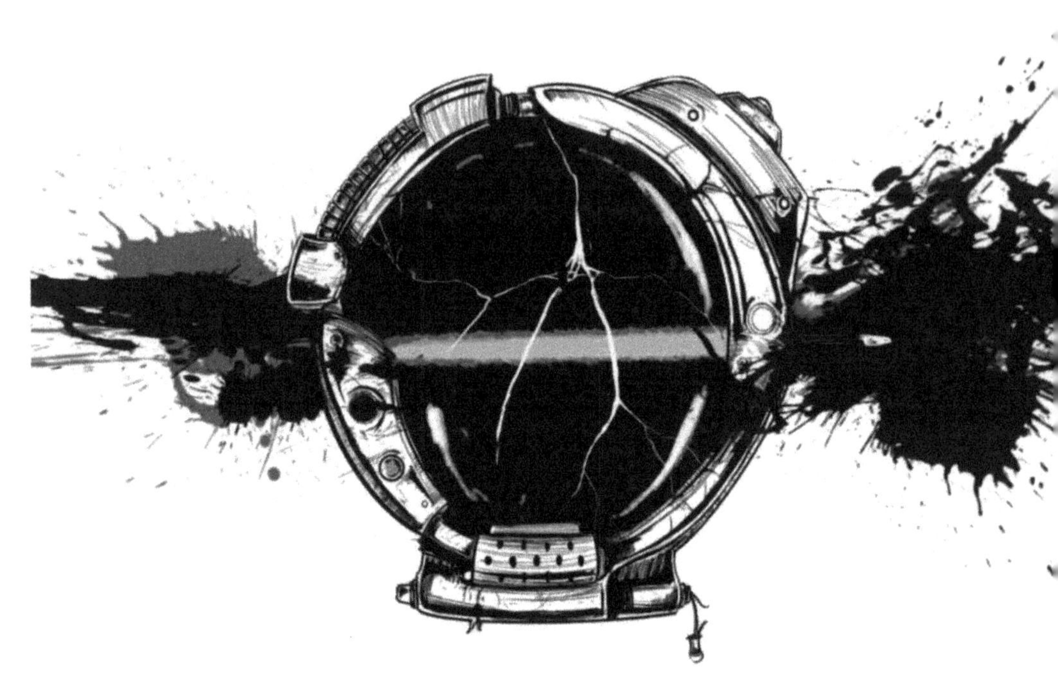

June 21, 2020:

Someone has to know what happened. The problem is... everyone seems to be an expert these days. When the end result is unbelievable, how do we know what is fact and what is fiction? Time to see how many theories are out there.

Note: what does this mean?

Writer/Letterer - Laurie Calcaterra

Pencils/Inks - Marco Defillo

Colors - Matt D. Chambers III

Editor - Rachael Bulock

YAWN
GOOD MORNING, MOM.
COFFEE, THANK YOU.
GASP!
JUDE, WHAT?!
ASL
CRASH

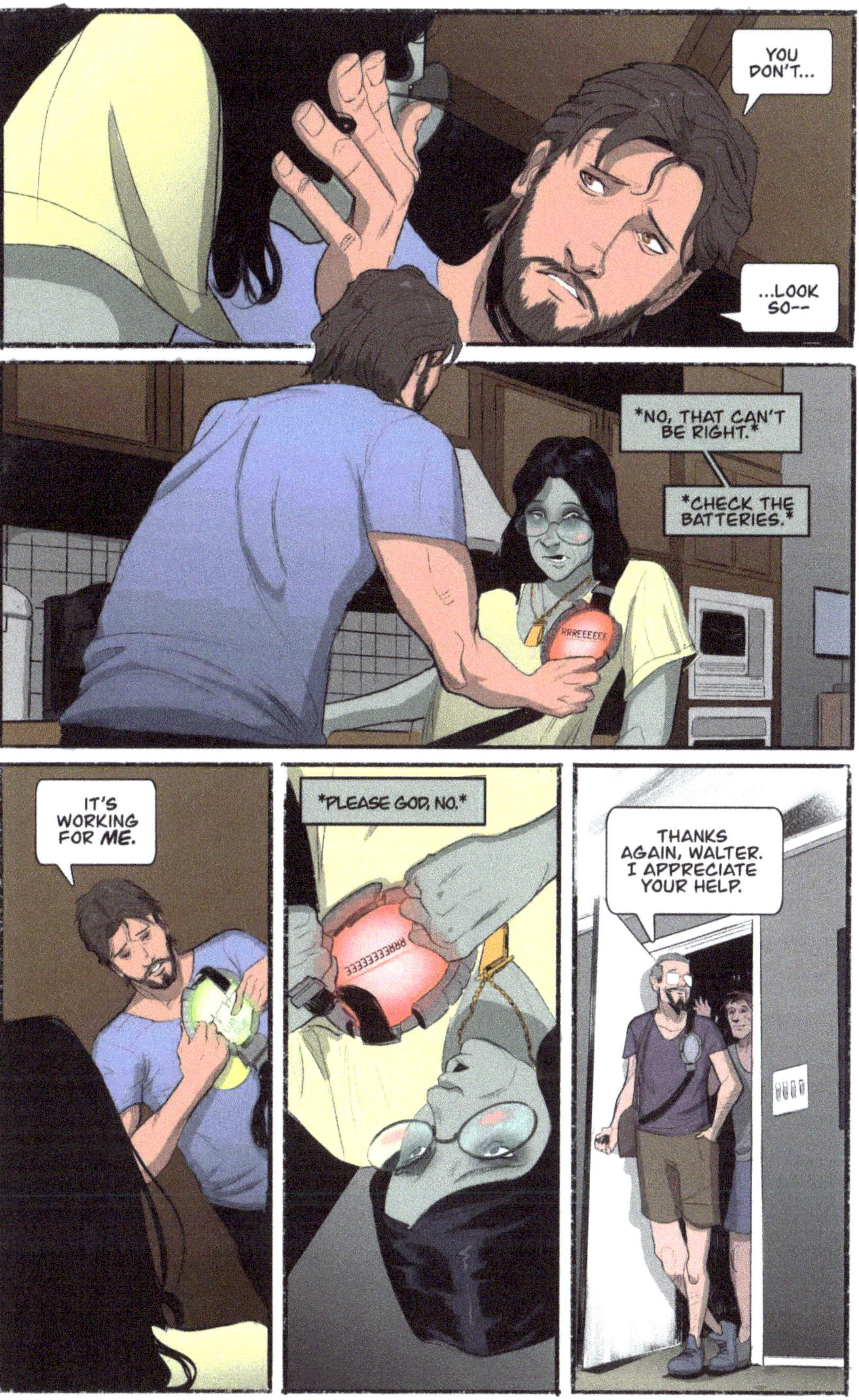

YOU DON'T...
...LOOK SO--

NO, THAT CAN'T BE RIGHT.
CHECK THE BATTERIES.
RRREEEEEEE

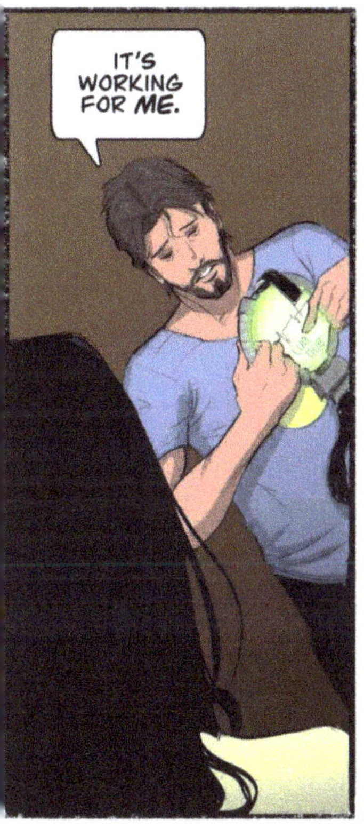

IT'S WORKING FOR ME.

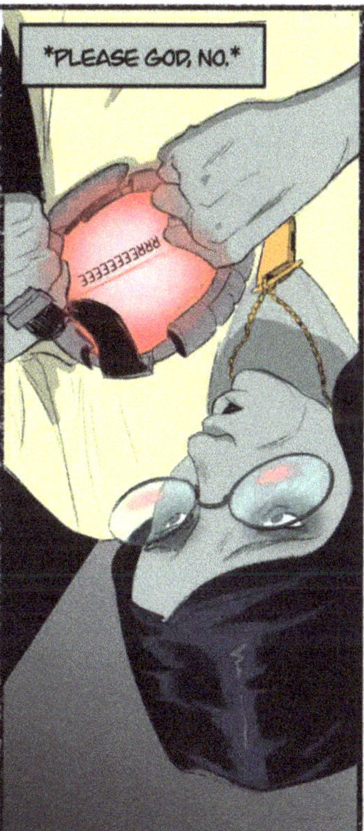

PLEASE GOD, NO.
RRREEEEEEE

THANKS AGAIN, WALTER. I APPRECIATE YOUR HELP.

I COULDN'T FIND A REPLACEMENT PART FOR THE TRUCK. YOU'RE A LIFESAVER.
COME ON IN. I CAN AT LEAST MAKE YOU A CUP OF COFFEE.
RIGHT THIS... ERM --

OOPS!

REALLY? OH, OK.
YOU KNOW WHAT? I JUST REMEMBERED I NEED TO RUN BACK OUT.

SILLY ME, I TOTALLY FORGOT.
UH-HUH. BYE!
RAIN CHECK ON THE COFFEE?

PHEW.

I CAN'T GO. I CAN'T.
NO ONE WILL BE ABLE TO UNDERSTAND ME.
I WILL BE ALL ALONE.
SHHH. MY LOVE YOU WILL NEVER BE ALONE.
YOU ARE GOING TO BE SAFE...
...HERE WITH US.
WE WILL ALWAYS PROTECT YOU.
REEF
REEEEEE

TWO WEEKS LATER
I BET SHE'S IN THE BATHROOM AGAIN.
MOM?
JUDE, WHO IS THIS?
WHO?
THE LADY IN THE WINDOW.
I KEEP WAVING...
...BUT SHE WON'T ANSWER.
SIGH... IT'S OK MOM.
COME AND KNIT ON THE COUCH.
YOU REMEMBER HOW TO KNIT, RIGHT?

Dear viewers, the west coast has been demolished.
From San Diego to Portland, cities have been burnt to the ground.
CC
The Undead Underground has made everything past the Rocky Mountains impassable. The further west you go, the less likely you will keep your heartbeat. The Undead dislike cold, so as we move towards the end of the year, head north to avoid violent encounters.
TAP
TAP
I KNOWS THAT GOLD IS BEHIND THIS.
HE SNARED DEATH OR MY NAME ISN'T DWAYNE FINK.
SCRIBBLE
Knock
Knock
THAT'S THE DOOR.

GOOD AFTERNOON. IS THIS THE ST. CLAIR HOME?
YES, IT IS.

WE HAVE ORDERS TO CHECK THE RESIDENCE FOR A HIDDEN UD.
ARE YOU THE ONLY ONE WHO LIVES HERE?
NO, SIR. IT'S MY FATHER AND I.

IS HE CURRENTLY HOME?
NO — ERR... HE'S NOT.

YOU MIND IF WE TAKE A LOOK SEE?
WELL, I --

WHAT'S THIS?
DINING ROOM CLEAR.

A DIARY... AND KNITTING?
YOU SURE NO ONE ELSE LIVES HERE?

UPSTAIRS IS CLEAR.

HEY JUDE, WHAT'S THE VAN--

IDENTIFY YOURSELF!
HEY! WHAT'S THIS ABOUT?!

I WILL END YOU!
STAND DOWN.
PHEW.
THIS MAN IS CLEARLY ALIVE.
EVERYTHING SEEMS IN ORDER.
WE WILL JUST - BE --
NO!
YOU CAN'T TAKE HER!
YOU WON'T.
CALL FOR BACK UP!

DON'T DO THIS!
SHE'S DEAF! SHE WON'T BE ABLE TO COMMUNICATE!
WE HAVE TO TAKE HER FOR THE SAFETY OF THE COMMUNITY.
SHE'S NOT A THREAT! SHE CAN STAY INSIDE!

Put the gun down or I will shoot you!

NO! JUST --
SIR! LET GO!

MAKE A GOOD CHOICE, NOW!
THERE IS ONLY ONE CHOICE.

TSK, TSK.
NOW YOU CAN GO TOGETHER.
BRREE!

TWO FOR THE PRICE OF ONE.
OK, LOOK AT ME.
JUDE, IT'S GOING TO BE OK.
TIME TO STAND ASIDE, SON.
YOU DON'T HAVE TO DIE TODAY.
JUDE. LET US GO. LIVE YOUR LIFE.
MOM, I CAN'T --
DON'T WORRY. YOUR DAD AND I WILL BE TOGETHER.
DON'T STOP FIGHTING. YOU CAN FIGURE THIS OUT.
WAIT... I --
I LOVE YOU.
SCREECH

MOM SAID FIGURE IT OUT.

ALL PACKED. NO POINT IN STAYING NOW.
PLOP

I'VE GOT A FULL TANK OF GAS, A BOOK FULL OF CONSPIRACY THEORIES AND THE AUDACITY TO CHASE A MIRACLE.
WHAT COULD GO WRONG?

AAAAAA!
ZZZZ...
CRASH

UNDEAD
UNDERGROUND
YAAAAA!
BRAAKA
BRAAKA
BRAAKA
AY DEA
WE

SHIT, THAT
TANK WENT FAST.

MAYBE I CAN
FIND A REFILL
HERE?
THIS
LOOKS LIVELY.

THIS IS AN UNLAWFUL GATHERING.
PLEASE SEGREGATE AND ALLOW THE UNDEAD TO BE COLLECTED.
ACTIVATE YOUR DISC TO FACILITATE THE PROCESS.
DEAD OUTSIDE
STILL HUMAN INSIDE!
STILL HUMAN INSIDE!
STILL HUMAN INSIDE!
STILL HUMAN INSIDE!
STILL HUMAN INSIDE!
STILL HUMAN INSIDE!
UN DEAD WANTED
STILL HUMAN INSIDE!
STILL HUMAN INSIDE!
YOU SHOULD THROW YOUR DISC.
YAAAAA!
YOU BASTARD!
BONK
TAKE COVER!
FUCK YOU, PO-PO!
TAKE THAT!
COLLECTOR CUNT!

WHY CAN'T THEY JUST LET EVERYONE BE?
PEOPLE ARE AFRAID. WE ARE DIFFERENT AND DIFFERENT IS DANGEROUS.
NO, PEOPLE ARE PEOPLE. UNDEAD ARE FRIENDS, FAMILY, AND NEIGHBORS IN MY BOOK.
COMPLY!
IS THAT WHY YOU CARRY IT WITH YOU?
MY JOURNAL? OH. I USED THIS TO KEEP TRACK OF IMPORTANT THINGS. THEORIES.
I'M HOPING TO FIND OUT WHAT CAUSED THIS.
WHAT ARE YOUR PLANS?
RESIST. THEY CAN'T COLLECT US ALL.

GEEK OUT

D&D, TABLETOP GAMES, COMICS, BOOKS & COLLECTIBLES

A PLACE LIKE NO OTHER THAT PROVIDES EVERYONE WITH A SAFE SPACE TO COME IN AND GEEK OUT!

20+ FREE TO PLAY TABLES

2 LOCATIONS IN THE DALLAS/FT. WORTH METROPLEX

YOUR HOME TO COLLECT AND ENJOY ALL OF YOUR FAVORITE BOARD GAMES, TABLE TOP GAMES, TRADING CARD GAMES, COMICS, MODELS, COLLECTIBLES AND MORE!!

 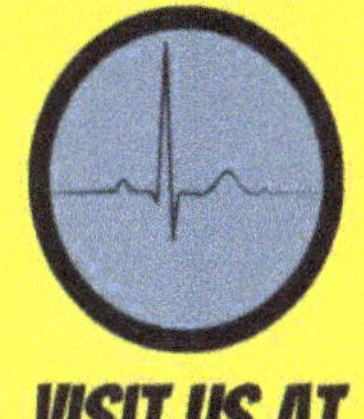 

109 WEST ELLISON ST	1509 FM 157
BURLESON, TX 76028	MANSFIELD, TX 76063
817-439-9777	682-400-8322

WWW.GEEKOUTTX.COM

OFFICIAL SPONSOR OF MANSFIELD BARRACUDAS HOCKEY

AN OFFICIAL PLAY SPACE OF FORT WORTH GAME NIGHT

LAST CHANCE!
DEPLOY ON 3.
ONE...
...TWO...
...THREE!
WHIRRRRR
CLICK
SNIKT
FFT
WHIMPER
FFFT
ARGHHH!
SNIK

FFFT
FFFT
FFFT
FFFT
FFFT
FFFT
FFFT
FFFT
RUN!
MARY!
GO!
MOVE!
RUN!
GO!
GO!
RUN!
MOVE!
GO!
HURK
SNIKT
FFFT
GASP
SNIKT
AAAAAAAAAAAAAAAAA!

GASP!
SMACK
FFFT
FFFT
FFFT
FFFT
FFFT

TIME TO GO!

AAAAAAAA
GASP
AIEEEE
DON'T LOOK BACK! JUST RUN!

ELECTRICAL ARC ACTIVATED.
BOOP

AIEEEE
Zzzt
Zzzt
Zzzt
Zzzt
Zzzt
GASP!

Zzzt
QUICK! IN HERE!

OH GOD! WHAT DID THEY DO?!
ALL THOSE PEOPLE! ALL MY PEOPLE!

GOT A LIVE ONE, HERE.
ZZZ ZZZt
AAAAAA!

CHECKING THE GROCERY.
OH NO!

HURRY! HIDE IN THE FREEZER!

C'MON OUT AND PUT YOUR HANDS UP!

TURN AROUND AND HIT THAT DISC!

I'M ALIVE, SIR!

ARE YOU A FILTHY SYMPATHIZER?
NO SIR, JUST OBSERVING.
ANY UD'S ON THE PREMISE?
NO, SIR. JUST ME.

I'LL CHECK FOR MYSELF, THANKS.
BE MY GUEST.

OK TROUBLEMAKER, MOVE OUT.
IF I CATCH YOU IN THIS TOWN AGAIN THERE WILL BE CONSEQUENCES.
YES, SIR!

DING DING
ASSHOLE.

IT'S SAFE NOW.
THUMP THUMP

I HATE THE COLD. IT MAKES ME THINK SLOW.

THEY'RE GONE. WHERE WILL YOU GO?
I'M NOT SURE. IT SEEMS ALL MY GROUP GOT COLLECTED EXCEPT FOR ME.
WELL, YOU CAN'T GIVE UP.
IF I WERE YOU, I WOULD DO ANYTHING TO NOT GET COLLECTED.
NO
DIXIE

KEEP FIGHTING? WHY DO YOU CARE?
MY MOM WAS COLLECTED A COUPLE MONTHS AGO.
OH, GOD. I'M SO SORRY TO HEAR THAT.
SHE WASN'T READY TO GO AND MY DAD WELL...
...HE DECIDED TO GO WITH HER.
I NEED TO BELIEVE THAT SOMEONE IS OUT THERE FIGHTING FOR THEM.
I DIDN'T. I FROZE. THE BEST I CAN DO NOW IS TRY TO FIGURE OUT THE "WHY".

WHAT'S YOUR NAME?
JUDE ST. CLAIR.
WELL JUDE, THANK YOU FOR SAVING ME TODAY. MY NAME IS LOLA MARTINEZ.
HERE'S HOPING YOU STAY ALIVE LONG ENOUGH TO FIGURE OUT THE "WHY".

THANKS. SPEAKING OF, HAVE YOU HEARD OF A GUY NAMED DWAYNE FINK OR THE GOLDEN CITY?
DWAYNE DOESN'T RING A BELL, BUT I HAVE HEARD A RUMOR ABOUT THE GOLDEN CITY.

IT'S SUPPOSEDLY A HAVEN FOR THE LIVING AND MY KIND HAVE BEEN TOLD TO STEER CLEAR FOR OUR OWN GOOD. THE UNDEAD RETIREMENT COMMUNITY IS NEARBY AND THAT'S JUST BEGGING TO BE COLLECTED. NOT SAFE.
I'VE HEARD RUMORS OF A GOLDEN MAN, THE FOUNTAIN OF YOUTH, ALL SORTS OF THINGS. I'M HEADING THAT WAY TO SORT THROUGH ALL THE HEARSAY AND UNCOVER THE TRUTH. IT'S OUT THERE, I CAN FEEL IT.
THOSE ALL SOUND MADE UP TO ME. BUT... HERE WE ARE. ARE YOU PLANNING ON WALKING ALL THAT WAY?

WELL... I JUST RAN OUT OF GAS. NOT MUCH CHOICE.
IT'S GOING TO TAKE YOU YEARS TO GET THERE.
ANYWAYS, I'M GOING TO SNEAK AROUND BACK.
OH, AND JUDE?
GOOD LUCK.
UM... THANKS, LOLA.
DON'T GIVE UP THE FIGHT.

A GOOD OLD FASHIONED MAP.

LET'S SEE... AH.

HERE YOU ARE.
SANTA-CLAUS

SO MUCH FOR FILLING UP GAS.
SIGH... LOLA IS RIGHT. IT'S GOING TO TAKE ME YEARS TO GET TO ARIZONA.
I JUST HAVE TO PACK AS MUCH AS I CAN CARRY AND START WALKING.
NOT MUCH LEFT OF THE WINDY CITY ANYWAYS.

CRUNCH
ER...
HI?
WHAT THE
HELL WAS THAT
THING?
TIME TO GO,
THINGS ARE
GETTING CREEPY
AROUND HERE.
SANTA
CLAUS, HERE
I COME.

SOCIAL MEDIA LINKS:

GET UPDATES AND ENGAGE THE CHAOS

YouTube: @lauriecalcaterra360

FACEBOOK GROUP: PATH OF THE PALE RIDER

INSTAGRAM: @PATH_OF_THE_PALE_RIDER

TWITTER: @PATHPALERIDER

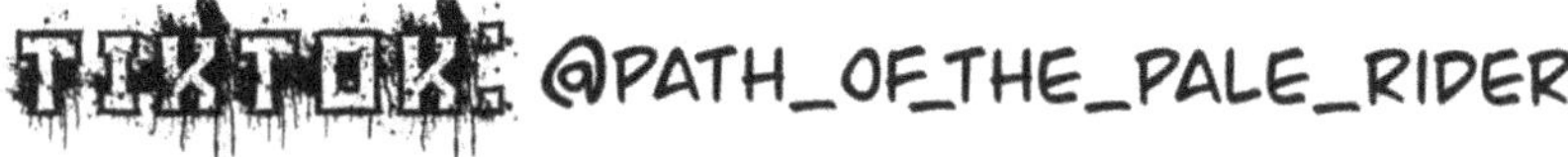

TIKTOK: @PATH_OF_THE_PALE_RIDER

WEBSITE: WWW.PATHOFTHEPALERIDER.COM

Follow Jude St. Clair in PATH OF THE PALE RIDER - Issue #5 coming soon!

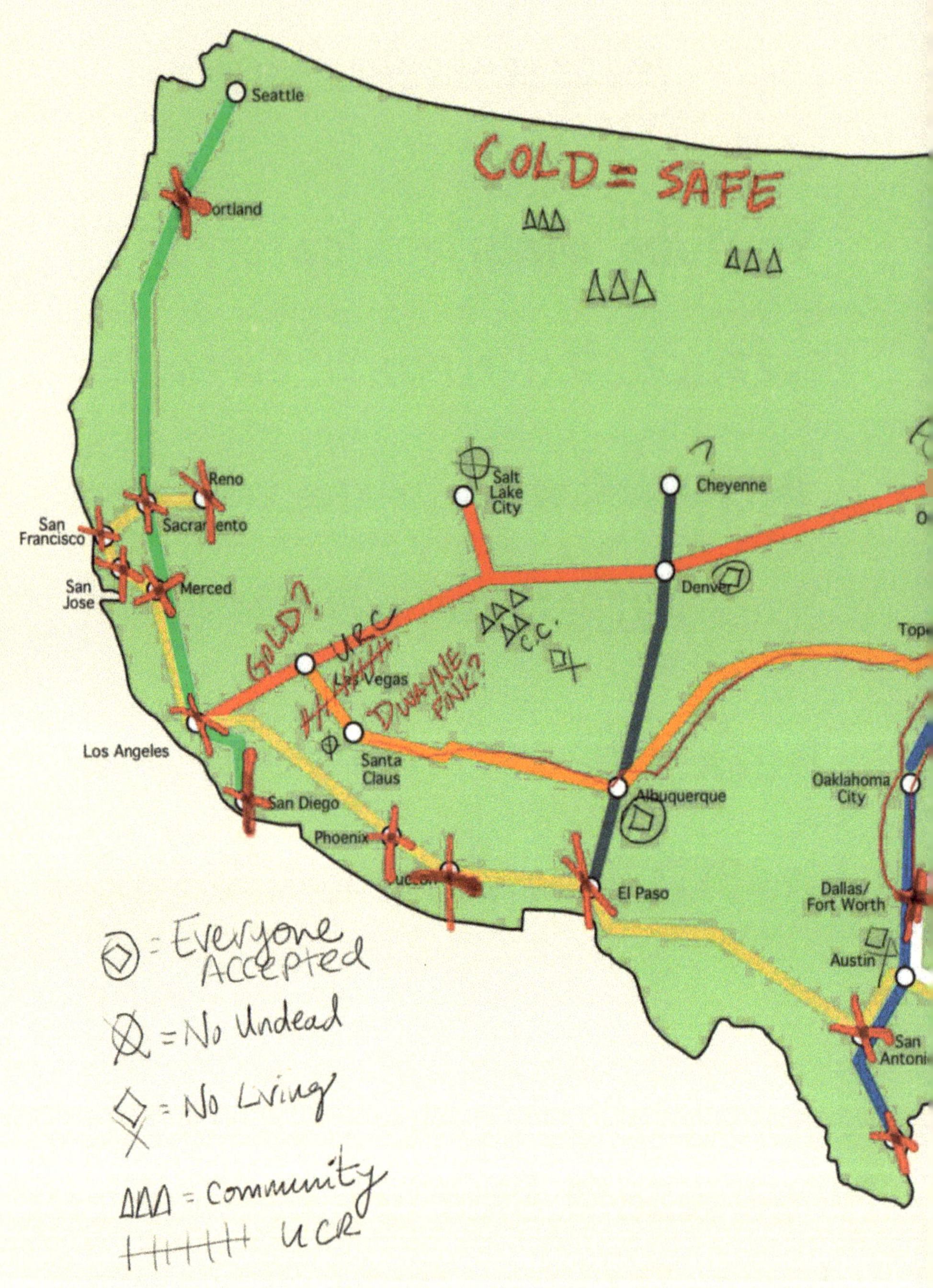

Seattle
Portland
COLD = SAFE
△△△
△△△
△△△
Reno
Sacramento
San Francisco
San Jose
Merced
Salt Lake City
Cheyenne
Denver
Topeka
GOLD?
URC
Las Vegas
DWAYNE PINK?
△△△
△△
C.C.
Los Angeles
Santa Claus
Oklahoma City
San Diego
Phoenix
Tucson
El Paso
Albuquerque
Dallas/Fort Worth
Austin
San Antonio
◎ = Everyone Accepted
⊘ = No Undead
◇ = No Living
△△△ = Community
╫╫╫ UCR

Montreal
Ottowa
Minneapolis
Albany
Portland
Milwaukee
Toronto
Boston
Detroit
Des Moines
Chicago
Cleveland
New York
Indianapolis
Philadelphia
Pittsburgh
Baltimore
maha
Columbus
Washington D. C.
Quincy
Cincinnati
Richmond
eka
Kansas
City
St. Louis
Louisville
Charlotte
Raleigh
Nashville
Memphis
Little
Rock
Atlanta
Charleston
Birmingham
Savannah
Mobile
Tallahassee
Jacksonville
Houston
New
Orleans
Orlando
West Palm
Beach
Miami

GOVERNMENT INVOLVEMENT

This is a big one. Probably the most dangerous to research. I'm finding people claiming all sorts of Govt foul play and then the videos disappear or the people mysteriously go missing. Nano tech, human experimentation, DNA mapping, deep brain electrical stimulation... It all sounds like science fiction, but again, here we are. Let's be careful with this one.

CONTAMINATED FOOD

This one has some interesting points. Contaminated food could have a simultaneous world wide response, but contaminated with what? No one seems to be able to identify anything that would have such an effect on humanity. More research needed.

Mushrooms?

VIRUS

Internet experts say it's a virus that started in the USA. That it's a mutated version of "wasting disease" we've seen in deer for decades. According to this theory it has jumped to every known creature, spread in the blood. What I haven't seen is anyone identify it through testing or samples. This needs more proof.

THE RAPTURE

A ton of people think this is some sort of spiritual awakinging or they missed the rapture. They claim God took the faithful to heaven and we were all left behind. But I didn't see anyone missing. Videos have surfaced of whole churches of every denomination gathering to pray. So none of them were faithful? Or heaven is full and no one else can get in? People are vocal about this one and I'm gathering info.

ALIENS

Another crazy idea. The greys? The greens? There's a circulating theory that aliens brought humans to earth, let us cultivate it for resources and now that we are too prolific, have introduced a mutigen to eradicate us. Like they want to clean house and move back in? I've found blurry videos online with UFO's and the like. Not sure this one is w researching.

UNDEAD UNDERGROUND

A resistance group has popped up. They compromise of Undead and Living sympathizers. Their goal? To save undead from collection. They provide guidance to the recently deceased from self embalming, hacking discs, symbols for friendly towns, and even safe houses to hide. I'm concerned this could escalate to something else. Look at what I found online:

UNDEAD PRESERVATION

This is wild. Undead are visiting FIXERS. They replace their blood with formaldehyde and get a coat of poly with paint. FIXERS are saying they can stay in their body longer. Maybe this will work? What other options do they have? As long as their brain is firing on all synapses, they won't spiral down into that chaos.

Cacophony awaits us all in the end.

Laurie Calcaterra • Marco Defillo
PATH OF THE
PALE RIDER
NO. 1

PATH OF THE
PALE RIDER
1
CALCATERRA ■ DEFILLO ■ RODRIGUEZ

PATH
OF THE
PALE RIDER
DEAD
END
1
CALCATERRA ∎ DEFILLO ∎ MARTINEZ

PATH OF THE
PALE RIDER
NO. 2
Laurie Calcaterra   Marco Defillo

PATH OF THE PALE RIDER

CALCATERRA ■ DEFILLO ■ RODRIGUEZ

PATH OF THE
PALE RIDER
2
CALCATERRA
DEFILLO
WATKINS
WELCOME SANTA CLAUS

PATH OF THE
PALE RIDER
2
CALCATERRA DEFILLO PEROTTA

PATH OF THE
PALE RIDER
CALCATERRA   DEFILLO   SALINAS 2

PATH OF THE
PALE RIDER
NO.3
BIG JAMES
CALCATERRA DEFILLO CHAMBERS

PATH OF THE
PALE RIDER
DEAD OUTSIDE
STILL HUMAN
INSIDE!
NO RISE
NO
RIGHTS
CALCATERRA
DEFILLO
CHAMBERS
AQUINO
3

PATH OF THE
PALE RIDER
CALCATERRA DEFILLO CHAMBERS WATKINS
3

PATH OF THE PALE RIDER

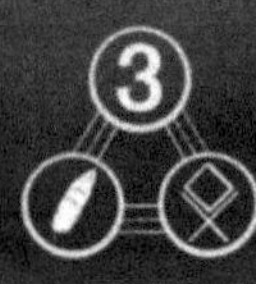

CALCATERRA DEFILLO CHAMBERS SANCHEZ

PATH OF THE
PALE RIDER
CALCATERRA DEFILLO CHAMBERS RUSSELL
3

PATH OF THE PALE RIDER

PATH OF THE PALE RIDER

CALCATERRA DEFILLO CHAMBERS KRUEGER

PATH OF THE
PALE RIDER
CALCATERRA DEFILLO CHAMBERS RUSSELL

PATH OF THE PALE RIDER

CALCATERRA DEFILLO CHAMBERS GIBSON

<u>PATH OF THE PALE RIDER</u>

WRITTEN BY

LAURIE CALCATERRA

2018

PATH OF THE PALE RIDER - EPISODE 1 - INTO THE THE WILD

EXT. DAYTIME - HILLY COUNTRY

Jude St. Clair is seen from far away, riding his horse,
Prince, a tan horse with a dark mane and tail. Jude is in
his mid to late 30s, with tanned skin, short scruffy beard,
and a fit build. He is wearing faded jeans, cowboy boots,
ripped cowboy hat and a plaid flannel shirt with the
sleeves rolled up to below his elbows. A gun belt is on
his hip, the handle of the gun is worn, showing use. The
horse is laden with bags, a bed roll, rifle, canteen, and
other essentials. The opening shows our hero traversing
through different terrain. First is a hilly empty space,
then abandoned burnt out cities and overgrown
infrastructure.

EXT. DAYTIME - ABANDONED TOWN

Jude is riding through an abandoned town. All the
buildings are empty, roads are dusty. There are cars
abandoned on the roads, doors left open. He warily looks
around for anything, his hand on the hilt of his gun. He
leans forward and whispers into the ear of his horse, she
slows down. You see a slight figure dart between the
camera and our hero, it draws his attention, he pulls his
gun from the holster. The figure is hiding partially
behind a car. Jude lowers his gun, taps a disc on his
chest. It flashes light to the beat of his heart and
amplifies the sound; bump-bump, bump-bump. The figure
steps out, it is a young man, skin and bones skinny. He
taps his disc, and it lights up as well.

                    JUDE
              Which way to I-93?

The youth points at the direction of the woods in the
distance. Jude puts his gun away, tips his hat and nudges
Prince to head towards the dense woods.

EXT. NIGHT - WOODS

Jude has set up a modest camp in a small clearing. Prince
is tied loosely to a tree, there is a fire burning. A slow
and gentle snow is coming down around him. The night is
dark and Jude feeds another log onto the fire and sits on a
stump. He watches the fire for a moment, then takes a
large journal out of his bag. He opens it and is reading a
page filled with handwriting and drawings. For a moment
the clouds clear and the small camp is filled with a cool
light from the moon. He gazes up at the bright stars in
adoration, the journal is forgotten. Suddenly, a twig
snaps behind him and Jude jumps. Standing quickly, he
drops the book and pulls a burning log from the fire and
brandishes it like a weapon in front of him, searching the
darkness. The howling of wolves is heard and eyes reflect
back the flickering fire light. One, two, five pairs of
eyes blink back at him. He turns in a slow circle with the
burning weapon, watching for movement, but the eyes blink
out and nothing comes forward. A howl is heard in the
distance.

EXT. MORNING - NARROW ROAD LEAVING THE WOODS

Jude is on top of Prince, slumped in the saddle. Obviously
tired, Jude gives an exaggerated yawn. The road is
crumbling and Prince stumbles and then catches herself.
They go around a bend and see a small house with a half
stone wall built around the property. In the yard is a
mother, early 30s, hair pulled up into a bun with wisps of
curly hair escaping her updo. She is wearing a worn shirt
and dirty pants, kneeling in front of a wooden trough
filled with dirt. She is tending a small vegetable garden.
From behind a large tomato plant, a small girl, around 6
years old, is warily watching Jude approach. Jude stops
with plenty of space between himself and the wall so not to
startle the woman and clears his throat to announce his
presence, climbs off his horse.

                    JUDE
          Hello, Ma'am. I don't want to
          startle you. I'm just looking for
          the road that leads to Santa Claus.

                    WOMAN
          Santa Claus? Aren't you a little
          old to believe in such things?

                    JUDE
          Not the legend, Ma'am. The town. I
          heard there is a town named Santa
          Claus in this area.

                    WOMAN
               (warily)
          And what takes you to this town?

                    JUDE
          I'm looking for a person. Dwayne
          Fink is his name. You familiar? He
          may have information I'm looking
          for.

                    WOMAN
          I'm sorry, I can't help you there.
          There is a small town at the top of
          the bluff a few miles up I-93.
          Could be the town, but the names
          have all been forgotten at this
          point.

                    JUDE
          Thank you, Ma'am. That's all I'm
          looking for is the direction and
          some hope. Can I trouble you for
          some water? I'm running low and I
          have quite a bit to travel before I
          can rest.

                    WOMAN
          I can do that for you, Traveler.
          Hand me your canteen and I will be
          right back.

The woman glances at the small girl.

                    WOMAN
               (Sternly)
          Sara, do not leave the yard.

The woman turns and walks into the house but is watching
her daughter through the window as she starts filling the
canteen. The girl glances behind her, then grabs some
carrots from a stack of vegetables and walks toward Jude
and Prince.

                    SARA
          Can I give your horsey a carrot,
          mister?

                    JUDE
          Hello Miss! My name is Jude St.
          Clair, and yes, Prince would love a
          carrot.

                    SARA
          I wish we had apples. I read in a
          book that he would prefer an apple.
          All I have is carrots.

                    JUDE
          Prince is actually a girl. Her
          full name is Diana Prince. Named
          after a warrior woman who was a
          protector of the human race.

                    SARA
          Hello, Diana! (Giggles) I have some
          extra carrots for you if you want
          one for the road.

                    JUDE
          Why thank you very much.

The girl hands a couple of carrots to Jude, reaches out a
hand and Prince nuzzles her gently. The girl giggles, but
her mother has come back and hands the canteen back to
Jude. The woman puts two hands on the girl's shoulders and
pulls her back towards the yard. Jude takes that as his
cue to get on his way. He climbs back on the horse, turns
to look back and the woman is tending to the tomatoes and
the girl is waving. He waves back and nudges Prince to
pick up the pace.

EXT. DAYTIME - THE BLUFF

Jude and Prince are at the bottom of the hilly road that nature has reclaimed. On their left, the black top is crumbling away, falling down the side of a cliff. The drop is about 50 feet before you see the tops of the trees below. On the right is a 50 foot bluff going up towards a hilltop. Jude stops Prince at the start of the curve and assesses their situation. He watches as a large chunk of earth dislodges from the cliff above, falls down and then careens off the cliff below with a thud as it hits the ground below the trees. Jude looks over the cliff from atop Prince's back with wide eyes. There is a large sign that looks like it was brought there. It is a rusted yellow sign that used to say DEAD END, but the END has been crossed of with red spray paint and replaced with red dripping letters: BEAR. The sign reads DEAD BEAR. Jude jumps off Prince's back and walks to her head.

                    JUDE
          What do you think, girl?

Prince whinnies.

                    JUDE
          I know, I know. We've gone so far,
          hard to turn back now. But… Bear?
               (Shrugs)

Prince stomps and Jude sighs.

                    JUDE
          Ok. But we will have to be quiet
          like we've practiced. Got it?

Jude pulls soft, round pouches from his bag and slips one after another over Prince's hooves to muffle the sound. Prince whinnies again and Jude hops on her back and off they go.

Jude and Prince are cautiously traveling down the crumbly
road, watching for falling rocks. They dodge boulders and
hug the road by the upwards cliff when possible, giving the
edge a wide berth. Jude and Prince are going around a
large fallen boulder with a hand and foot sticking out from
the side. The hand was still clasped around something and
is wriggling in endless torment. Jude bends down and yanks
a chipped glass out from the fingers. The glass comes out
from his grip and flies towards the edge of the cliff. Jude
leaps towards it, catching it with his fingertips. He is
lying on the road, arm extended over the edge with the
glass hanging from two fingers. He stands up, breathing
hard and heads back to Prince with his prize. He wipes the
accumulated dirt off the side and holds it up to the sky;
the map of Las Vegas visible. The etching is almost gone
from one side, but the words LAS VEGAS are still clear as
day. He pulls a bandana out from his saddle bag, wraps the
glass carefully. A crow calls out and Jude realizes where
he is again and shoves the glass into the top of his pack,
still peeking out from the top. They go around a sharp
turn and stop. A large black mass is lying all the way
across the road. It's furry and there is a massive swarm
of flies surrounding the carcass. Five or six large crows
pick at the mass, dipping their beaks into the flesh
pulling out sinew. Jude slides off Prince's back silently.
He comes close to her head and whispers in her ear. Prince
nods and they proceed very slowly towards the dead thing.
As they get closer, they see it is indeed a bear. The
black bear has matted hair, eyes a glossy grey, half open
and staring. A large scar covers it's right eye. It's
throat is torn open and flies crawl in its gaping mouth;
tounge lolling to the side with maggots crawling. Jude
leads Prince towards the edge where the bear's feet are 12
inches from the precipice. He guides Prince's feet, one at
a time over the bear's sprawling legs; careful not to touch
any part of the rotten remains. They succeed in getting
around the obstacle and continue as quietly as possible.
Jude is walking along side of Prince. They continue
straight on the road, behind them is the unmoving bear.
Prince stumbles in a small hold and the glass come loose.
Jude watches it fall in slow motion, reaching for it but
the glass is out of reach. Jude freezes with the sound of
breaking glass; eyes wide. He moves a quick hand to
Prince's neck and she freezes. They stand perfectly still,

waiting to see if the noise changes their situation. Jude
turns his head slowly, but the bear is still across the
road. He turns back around and sighs, but the hairs on his
neck stand up. Behind him, the silhouette of a five-
hundred-pound bear is standing upright. The bear roars and
Jude turns to see it in all its cold dead fury. He jumps
on Prince's back and yells.

                         JUDE
                GO!!!!!

The bear is chasing them down the road. Prince is running
as fast as she can muster down the dilapidated blacktop,
jumping over rocks and logs in her way. Jude is
encouraging her, but the bear is getting closer. Prince
makes it off the bluff, and the forest is creeping up
again, the path is dirt. Jude glances behind them and the
bear is still gaining.

                         JUDE
                RUN, PRINCE! GO GO GO!

Prince is running at full speed, but the bear is upon them,
swipes at Prince's back feet, knocking Jude off and
scattering their belongings from her back. Prince is
screaming and the bear is on top of her, ripping her to
shreds. Jude is unconscious, in the brush, bleeding from a
head wound.

                                        CUT TO BLACK

EXT. NIGHT - END OF THE TWISTY ROAD

Jude wakes up slowly, looking around. He remembers the
bear and crouches close to the ground while he gets his
bearings. He has a cut on the side of his head that bled a
bit. He winces as he put his hand against the cut. His
fingers come away bloody, but it's not serious. In the
darkness, he can see lights in the distance. He slowly
stands, searching the area for Prince and his belongings.
There is a large pool of blood in the middle of the path,
but Prince is nowhere to be found. He kneels for a few
seconds, touching the ground close to the blood, head down
while he mourns his companion. His saddle bag is at the
edge of the road. He opens it, pulls out his wallet, his
journal, and his canteen. He pulls up his gun belt, throws
his bag over his shoulder and walks towards the town. He

hears the bear roar in the distance and pushes his hat onto
his head with one hand and runs towards the town, not
looking back.

                                        END

INT. MORNING - JUDE'S PARENTS HOUSE

Picking up where we left off, Mom "wakes up" Undead. She stretches and yawns, gets up, folds the blanket and lays it neatly on the back of the couch. She heads to the kitchen and starts the coffee machine. Jude walks in and signs good morning to her. She hands him a cup of coffee and he gets his first good look at her. He drops his coffee cup, which shatters on the floor. She looks at him perturbed.

> MOM
> What the heck, Jude?!

> JUDE
> (Panicked) Mom, come here!

She comes closer and Jude grab her face, looks closer at her eyes, then frantically turns on her disc, which does nothing. She looks at it and frowns.

> MOM
> That can't be right. Check it's
> batteries.

Jude snatches the disc off his mother's chest and puts it on himself, it lights up immediately, green-green to the beat of his heart.

> MOM
> No! That's not… It CAN'T be.

She snatches the disc back and puts it on her chest. After a 3 second pause, a red light comes on a stays on.

> JUDE
> Just stay calm, Mom. I -

The back door to the garage opens and Dad walks in with neighbor, Walter close behind.

> DAD
> It's the least I can do for you,
> Walter! Have a cup of coffee with
> me. I appreciate you helping me
> fix… the -

Dad freezes in the doorway at the sight of Jude and Mom
looking like deer in the headlights. Walter bumps into Dad
since he did not expect him to stop so abruptly. Mom is
Undead with the disc light red. The light is *RED*. Dad
quickly assesses the situation and turns blocking Walter's
view of the kitchen.

>   DAD
>   Sorry, Walt, we will have to have a
>   rain check on that coffee! I just
>   remembered I need to run to town to
>   get something for Jude. Can I stop
>   by later? Maybe we can go out for a
>   burger?

>   WALTER
>   Oh? Ok. It's ok. I doubt the diner
>   has any beef anyways. Let's just
>   figure something out tomorrow.

>   DAD
>   Ok, bye now!

Walter is trying to peek around Dad to see what the issue
is. Dad slams the door in Walter's face. Dad locks the door
behind him, walks through the kitchen closing all the
blinds, then turns to his wife. She is silently crying. He
walks to her and embraces her; she sobs into his chest.
Jude walks up and puts his arms around both of them.

>   MOM
>   I don't want to go! I don't know
>   what I'm going to do. How will
>   they understand me?

>   DAD
>   Don't worry, my love. You will
>   never be alone. You will always be
>   safe. With us. We will protect you.

He lifts her face to his. She gives a teary eyed smile and
hugs him tighter. She takes her disc off and grips it
tightly.

INT. DAY - TV ROOM

TWO WEEKS LATER

Jude walking down the hallway, shades are nailed to the
window sills. He sees his mom in the bathroom, waving at
the mirror. Jude touches her shoulder from behind, she has
a confused look on her face.

                    JUDE
          Mom?

                    MOM
          Who is she?

                    JUDE
          Who?

                    MOM
          The woman in the window. I keep
          waving and asking her name. Maybe
          she doesn't understand.

                    JUDE
          Mom… that's you. This is a mirror.

Mom continues waving with distant look in her eyes.

                    JUDE
          Mom, let's go sit on the couch and
          knit for a bit. We can check the
          news.

Jude is sitting on the couch with a laptop propped up on
the couch beside him. Mom sits in a chair across from him,
picking up knitting a scarf, which starts regular but then
becomes increasingly erratic as it continues. A haggard
looking Louis Landon is on television again, giving a news
report.

                    LOUIS LANDON
          The west coast has all been
          eliminated. From San Diego all the
          way up to Portland, cities have
          been burnt to the ground. The
          Undead Underground movement has
                    (MORE)

                    LOUIS LANDON (CONT'D)
          made everything past the Rocky
          Mountains impossible to get to. The
          further west you go, the less
          likely you will keep your
          heartbeat. Just a reminder that
          Undead dislike cold, so as we get
          towards the end of the year, head
          north to avoid violent encounters.

Jude is researching conspiracy theories on the web. One he
comes across has a short video of Dwayne Fink, saying he
met a man in the "City of Gold" who claims to have beaten
Death. When asked further questions, Dwayne asks for beer
money and the video ends. The news report is from Arizona.
As Jude writes down "Dwayne Fink, City of Gold, Arizona
- ???" In his notebook, there is a knock at the front door.
Jude gets up to answer. Mom looks up, Jude signs, "Door"
and "Hide" on his way out of the room.

INT. DAY - FRONT ENTRY OF JUDE'S PARENTS HOUSE

Jude opens the door and freezes as two men in black
official looking uniforms stand on the porch. They have the
badge of Collectors on their chest. Officer 1 is a tall
white man with jet black hair. He is muscular and has an
arrogance to the way he carries himself. Officer 2 is
 forgettable uniform. Nothing stands out about him.
 Officer 1 is in charge.

                    OFFICER 1
          Hello, is this the St. Clair
          residence?

                    JUDE
          (Trying to hide surprise) It is.

Officer 1 reaches up and activates the disc on Jude's shirt
without permission. It starts lighting up and beating
along with his heart.

                    OFFICER 1
          We have a report a UD is hiding in
          this residence. Are you the only
          one that lives here?

                    JUDE
          No Sir, it's me and my father.

                    OFFICER 1
          Is he currently home?

                    JUDE
          No Sir, he's off in town at the
          moment.

                    OFFICER 1
          Do you mind if we take a look
          around?

                    JUDE
          Actually, I -

But Officer 1 has already pushed Jude aside and is
strutting into the house. He walks through the kitchen
into the TV room. There is no one there. The knitting is
sitting on the corner of the couch. The collectors search
room by room, tossing things out of drawers and cabinets,
with Jude trailing behind, trying to stay calm. As they
are searching, the back door opens and Dad comes through.

                    DAD
          Hey, Jude! I saw a black van out
          front. Do you know if -

Officer 2 rushes over to Dad and flattens him against the
wall. His stomach and face are against the wall.

                    DAD
          HEY! What is this about?!

Officer 2 flips his body around so he can activate his
disc. It beats fast with his upset heartbeat.

                    OFFICER 2
          Clear.

                    OFFICER 1
          (To Officer 2) Stand down. (To Dad)
          Geez, man, you startled us.

The Officers step back from Dad, who is breathing heavily
and looking at Jude for any information, slightly panicked.
Jude shakes his head no very quickly. Officer 1 looks from

Dad to Jude and pauses, the anxiety is palpable. Then:

                         OFFICER 1
                Ok. Everyone accounted for here.

Officer 1 and 2 start walking back to the front door. They
pass the powder bath in the hallway. As they do, the door
opens and Mom comes out, having forgotten that there was a
search going on, due to memory loss and inability to hear.
Officer 2 is already out the front door on the sidewalk.
Officer 1 is in the open doorway, turns back to talk to
Dad, who walked him out. Dad and Jude are in between
Officer 1 and Mom. Officer 1 goes wide eyed as she comes
out the bathroom door. Dad looks back, sees Mom, then
turns back and grabs the side arm out from Officer 1's gun
belt and presses it against the Collector's forehead.
Officer 1 puts his hands up and looks cross-eyed at the
gun, surprised. Officer 2 comes back with gun drawn,
trying point it at Dad, but Officer 1's large body is
blocking the shot. Jude is blocking his mother with his
body.

                         OFFICER 1
                Don't do this, sir! We are only
                here to collect Cally St. Clair. We
                received a tip that she is hiding
                from collection.

                         DAD
                Please! You can't take her! She is
                deaf. She will have no way to
                communicate and it will be
                terrifying if I am not there to
                protect her!

                         OFFICER 2
                PUT THE GUN DOWN OR I WILL SHOOT
                YOU!

                         DAD
                She doesn't even leave the house!
                She is not a risk to anyone.

                    OFFICER 1
          That's not how this works and you
          know it, Sir! We have to take her
          for the safety of the community.

Officer 2 is on the walkie, calling for back up.

                    OFFICER 1
          Back-up is coming. There is
          nowhere for you to hide her. It's
          time. Put the gun down and let us
          take her, NOW!

With tears streaming down his face, jaw set, Dad's gun hand
is shaking against Officer 1's head. He abruptly turns the
gun on himself and shoots himself in the head. BLAM!

                    JUDE
          NOOOOO!

Dad falls down dead, a small hole from a gunshot on his
forehead and gore splashed on the wall behind him. Officer
1 sighs, putting his hands down and turns to Officer 2.

                    OFFICER 1
          Two for the price of one! Call off
          that back up. (Pointedly looking at
          Jude) We won't have any more
          problems, right Son?

He steps into the foyer where a pool of blood is growing
around Dad. He puts a hand on his face, looking at the
wound, shakes his head.

                    OFFICER 1
          Tsk, Tsk! Now you can go together.

Dad coughs and his cloudy eyes shift to focus on Officer 1.
Officer 1 offers him a hand, helping him up. Then he
roughly handcuffs him and shoves him towards Officer 2.
Officer 1 turns to the hallway where Jude and Mom are
crying. Jude is still blocking Mom.

                    OFFICER 1
          Stand aside, son.

Jude stands a bit straighter, with a serious look on his
face, but his mother puts a hand on his shoulder and steps
around him. She looks up at his face and signs to him:

                    MOM
          You need to let us go. Live your
          life!

                    JUDE
          (Just signing) I can't let you go!

                    MOM
          Don't worry, your Dad and I will be
          together. Don't stop fighting! You
          can figure this out. I love you.

Jude signs "I love you" and Mom walks towards Officer 1 who
cuffs her and escorts Mom and Dad out to the black panel
van. They are loaded into the back and Jude watches,
feeling helpless as they speed off. Jude looks over and
sees Walter quickly close his blinds.

EXT. MORNING - OUTSIDE JUDE'S PARENTS HOUSE

Jude is packing up his car with his belongings. He throws
his journal in the front seat and backs out of the
driveway. A "FREE HOUSE" sign is in the front window. The
neighborhood is already on fire as he pulls out of the
driveway and doesn't look back.

                              (PREVIOUSLY 5) RIOTS AND PURPOSE

EXT - DAY/NIGHT/DAY - CITIES AND TOWNS

TWO WEEKS LATER It's morning, Jude is adding adding the
last of the collected gas into the car.

                    JUDE
          Not enough. Won't be going far on
          this tank…

He looks around and there is a town in a few blocks away.
There is a large congregation of people holding signs. He
grabs his journal and locks up the car, heading toward the
group. The people are holding homemade signs above their

heads and chanting together. "Dead Outside" "Still Human Inside". Jude wanders into the crowd moving almost all the way to the front. There are wooden barriers separating the crowd from a group of Collectors. The town behind has a large sign "UNDEAD - UNWANTED" No one is moving past the barrier. Jude stops next to a petite Undead woman, who is chanting along with the group. Jude surveys the group, there are Living and Undead together. The Collectors are wearing riot gear and are lined up behind the wooden barriers. The Collector in charge is standing on top of a SUV with a megaphone.

                    COLLECTOR
          This is an unlawful gathering.
          Please segregate and allow the
          Undead to be collected. If you
          have a disc, please activate it to
          facilitate the process.

A figure with silver eyes wearing a hoodie and a face mask is standing next to a huge Undead protestor, casually leaning in and whispers into his ear. The large Undead man removes his disc and chucks it at the barricade line in defiance. The Collectors duck and scowl back at him. Then the protestors all start removing their discs one by one and throwing them at the Collectors, doing their best to hit them. The Collectors raise their clear plastic shields to avoid the onslaught.

                    JUDE
          Why can't they just let everyone
          be?

                    LOLA
          People are afraid. We are
          different and different is
          dangerous.

                    JUDE
          No, people are people. Undead are
          family, friends, and neighbors in
          my book.

                    LOLA
          Is that why you carry it with you?

                    JUDE
          The book? Oh. I just keep track of
          the things I think are important.
          I'm searching for the cause.

                    LOLA
          I'm not sure I follow.

                    JUDE
          Maybe if we figure out how this all
          started, we can put it right.

                    COLLECTOR
          This is your last warning!
          Dissipate and turn in the Undead
          for collection or there will be
          CONSEQUENCES.

                    JUDE
          (To Lola) What are you going to do?

                    LOLA
          Resist. They can't take us all
          down.

The figure in the hoodie is now on the side of the
collectors, his eyes shining silver in the low light. The
collectors are all reaching into their back pockets and
pulling out devices, pushing a red button and the smallish
disc snaps out sharp barbs. They are looking at the
Collector in charge and he counts down from three and they
all throw the items in unison. People scream in pain as the
weaponized discs imbed themselves into flesh. The blinking
light visible just under the skin. Jude deflects one from
Lola with his journal, sends it flying into the back of
another person running away, who stumbles and falls. He
grabs Lola by the arm and they run away from the chaos and
duck into a grocery store. They crouch as they push
through the broken glass of the front door. As soon as
they are through, they hear an electric hum as the
weaponized discs are activated. Electricity arcs from
screaming person to person, Living and Undead, eventually
rendering them all unconscious. They twitch and writhe on
the ground until they are still. Jude and Lola watch in

horror and look for a place to hide as the collectors have
started moving through the crowd with taser guns drawn.
They turn people over, checking the blinking light of the
small discs embedded in arms, backs, and necks. Green =
Living, Red = Undead. The Living are zip tied and dragged
to the curb. The Undead are zip tied and thrown into the
back of a black unmarked vans. Jude sees a deep freezer
and helps Lola climb in. Jude covers her with a towel and
heaps of bags of frozen peas on top. A Collector stops
inside the store just as Jude slams the top shut.

                    COLLECTOR
          (Taser drawn) Sir, activate your
          disc and put your hands up!

Jude activates his disc and puts his hands in the air. The
Collector makes note that the light is green.

                    JUDE
          I was just observing the crowd from
          here.

                    COLLECTOR
          Are you a sympathizer, sir?

                    JUDE
          No, sir. (Signing yes)

                    COLLECTOR
          Did you witness any UD's coming
          through the vicinity?

                    JUDE
          There was one that ran past the
          door, but they saw me and kept
          running. There isn't a warm body
          left in the store but me.

                    COLLECTOR
          I'll take a look for myself.

The Collector walks through the front of the store checking
behind registers and tipping over displays. He finds
nothing and heads back to Jude.

                         COLLECTOR
          Best if you move on, sir. Stay out
          of trouble.

Jude sighs, puts his hands down, and watches the Collector
head out and rejoin the ranks. The hooded figure is
standing just behind the Collector in charge, watching the
clean up. Jude taps his fingers on the freezer chest,
opening the top slowly and Lola climbs out.

                         LOLA
          Man, the cold makes me slow. I
          can't think straight.

                         JUDE
          They are leaving. Where will you
          go?

                         LOLA
          Not sure. It seems all of my group
          just got picked up except for me.

                         JUDE
          Don't give up the fight. If I were
          you, I would do ANYTHING to not get
          collected.

                         LOLA
          Keep fighting? And why do you care?

                         JUDE
          My mom was collected a couple weeks
          ago. She wasn't ready and my dad,
          well, he… decided to go with her.

                         LOLA
          I'm sorry to hear that.

                         JUDE
          Yeah. I need to believe someone
          out there is doing something for
          them. I couldn't. I froze. The
          best I can do is try to figure out
          the "why".

                    LOLA
What's your name?

                    JUDE
Jude. Jude St. Clair.

                    LOLA
Well Jude St. Clair, thank you for
saving me today. My name is Lola
Angustia. (They shake hands) Here's
hoping you stay alive to figure out
the "why".

Jude opens his journal, flips through some pages.

                    JUDE
Thank you. Speaking of, have you
heard of a guy named Dwayne Fink or
the Golden City?

                    LOLA
The name doesn't ring a bell, but I
have heard a rumor about the Golden
City. It's supposedly a haven for
the Living and my kind have been
told to steer clear for our own
good. The Undead Retirement
Community is nearby and that's just
begging to be collected. Not safe
for us.

                    JUDE
I've heard rumors of a Golden Man,
the fountain of youth, all sorts of
things. I'm heading that way to
sort through the all the hearsay
and uncover the truth. It's out
there, I can feel it.

                    LOLA
Those all sound made up to me. But…
here we are. Are you planning on
walking all that way?

                    JUDE
          Well… I am about to run out of gas.
          Not much choice.

                    LOLA
          It's going to take you years to get
          there. Anyways, I'm going to sneak
          out the back. And Jude… (winks)
          Good luck.

                    JUDE
          (Jude blushes and gives a puppy dog
          smile) Lola… you be safe as well.
          Don't give up the fight.

He watches her go; waves when she turns back to look at him
one last time. Jude heads to a stand by the front of the
grocery store, takes a map out of the rack. He opens it,
comparing his journal to the map, running his finger along
the red and blue lines. He heads out the door, back to his
car and finds that one of the tires is flat, being
punctured by a stray "weaponized disc".

                    JUDE
          Aw crap. Walking it is.

Grabbing as many things as he can, Jude heads down the
road, passing the barricade. The strange figure with the
hoodie and silver eyes is walking up ahead on the opposite
side of the road. Jude's footsteps in the gravel make the
figure stop. The two lock eyes for a second and the hairs
on the back of Jude's neck stand up. The silver eyes
staring back do not blink. Jude has a funny feeling that
the thing looking back is not human. The figure abruptly
turns and runs off the road into the desert scrub bushes
beyond and disappears into the night.

                    JUDE
          What is that THING?

Jude watches this strange figure fade into the night, sighs
a sigh of relief, glances up at the stars and heads off
down the road.

                                                  END